# SECRETS OF THE HEART

## BOOK ONE OF THE MACCALLENS AND RANDALLS

### SUZAN TISDALE

ISBN: 978-1-943244-49-2

## ALSO BY SUZAN TISDALE

### The Clan MacDougall Series

*Laiden's Daughter*

*Findley's Lass*

*Wee William's Woman*

*McKenna's Honor*

### The Clan Graham Series

*Rowan's Lady*

*Frederick's Queen*

### The Mackintoshes and McLarens Series

*Ian's Rose*

*The Bowie Bride*

*Rodrick the Bold*

*Brogan's Promise*

### The Clan McDunnah Series

*A Murmur of Providence*

*A Whisper of Fate*

*A Breath of Promise*

### Moirra's Heart Series

*Stealing Moirra's Heart*

*Saving Moirra's Heart*

### Stand Alone Novels

*Isle of the Blessed*

*Forever Her Champion*

*The Edge of Forever*

Arriving in 2019:

Black Richard's Heart

The Brides of the Clan MacDougall

(A Sweet Series)

*Aishlinn*

*Maggy*

*Nora*

*Arriving soon:*

*The MacAllens and Randalls Series*

*Secrets of the Heart*

*Tender is the Heart*

# INTRODUCTION

A few years ago, I wrote a very tiny story titled *The Thief's Daughter*, for a Christmas anthology. Onnleigh and Connor's story has been tumbling around in the back of my mind ever since.

Sometimes, the muse whispers sweetly in your ear, softly telling you the story that needs to be told. And sometimes, it screams at you. The story you are about to read was born of the latter sort.

I have added tons more content to this story and have retitled it, *Secrets of the Heart*. Onnleigh and Connor are going to launch an entirely new series for me, titled The MacCallens and Randalls. If the Lord is willing and the creek don't rise, I'll be releasing the next book in this series - *Tender is the Heart* — in a few months.

2019 is going to be an awesome year!

Hugs,

Suzan

*For GP Ching, Laurie Larsen, TM Cromer, Kate Bateman, and Sara Whitney.*

# PROLOGUE

## NOVEMBER 1425, THE HIGHLANDS, NEAR THE FORTH OF MORAY

*N*o one but her mum had ever called Onnleigh pretty. Thief, liar, wretched creature? Daughter of a drunkard and thief? Aye, she'd been called all those things, more times than she could count. But pretty? Nay, not pretty.

"I dunnae lie to ye, lass," Darwud MacCallen said as he sat next to the stream that helped feed Loch Moy. He was smiling at her as he played with a long blade of yellow grass. She stood in the stream trying to catch a fish for her supper. Though the water was frigid this time of year, fishing was a necessity, especially if she wanted to eat anything more than dried apples for her supper.

He was being so kind to her, something she was not accustomed to, especially from members of her clan. An outcast since the age of nine—all because of her father's love of drink and thieving—to have a young man like Darwud tell her how pretty he thought her, was more than unusual.

"Stop yer jestin', Darwud MacCallen," she told him as she waded farther into the cold water. She'd been in the stream for at least half an hour and had yet to catch anything. Darwud was a distraction she wasn't necessarily sure she wanted to go away.

He laughed, his crooked smile showing less than perfect teeth.

Darwud was not a handsome lad, but neither was he hideous or unappealing.

"Ye wound me, lass!" he said as he crossed one ankle over the other and tossed the blade away. "I would never lie to such a bonny thing as ye."

*Bonny? Pretty?*

He'd been coming around now and again for a few weeks, offering to help with her garden, her chickens and milk cow. He'd even been kind enough to help mend the thatched roof of the croft she shared with her father.

Standing in the center of the stream, with the hem of her dress tucked into her belt, she slipped an errant strand of hair behind her ear. *Bonny. Pretty.* How many times had he said such sweet things to her?

A large trout swam between her ankles, its tail fin just brushing her left foot. *Damnation!* she thought to herself. If she didn't focus on the task at hand, they'd be eating wild lettuce and berries for supper. "Why do ye say such things?" she asked, turning her attention back to the stream.

Before she knew it, he was wading into the water. "Let me help ye, lass."

Mayhap time had changed people. It had been years since she'd set foot anywhere near the MacCallen keep. Mayhap Darwud didn't know about her father, his reputation as a drunkard and layabout. Aye, all they said about her da was true she'd not deny it. But what they said of her? Not one word of it the truth. She never told a lie, hadn't stolen anything since she was nine, and worked very hard to keep home and hearth. She supposed it boiled down to what the Bible said about the sins of the father passing to the son and all that. Though she wasn't Grueber's son, she reckoned the good people of Clan MacCallen didn't care to make the distinction.

Darwud was standing next to her now, bent over at the waist, hands cupped under the cool water. "Now watch and see how I do it."

She resisted the urge to scoff at him. With a father as unreliable as

Grueber, she'd learned early in life how to fend for herself. That included fishing. Still, it was awfully kind of him to help.

A warm late autumn breeze flittered in over the tree-lined bank, caressing her skin, and pulling more of her unruly red hair out of her braid. Though she was trying to catch a fish, her mind was anywhere but on the matter at hand.

Moments passed by, with her heart happily dancing against her chest. Dare she believe that the rumors and stories had faded with time? Dare she hope that someone might take a fancy to her?

"Ah ha!" Darwud cried out as he scooped a large trout out of the water and held it up for her to see. It flipped and flopped, splashing little bits of water onto her nose. "That, my lass, is how it be done!" he exclaimed.

Why she clapped her hands together, she couldn't say. But she did. "That be a right good fish, Darwud!" she told him approvingly. "Da and I will give thanks to ye when we sit down to sup this night."

His expression changed from victorious to something far more mischievous. "Ye want the fish?" he asked.

She furrowed her brow in confusion. "Aye, I do. Did ye nae catch it fer me?" Embarrassment forced the color to creep up her neck, reddening her cheeks.

"Mayhap I did, mayhap I dinnae," he said as he headed toward the rocky bank.

Onnleigh remained standing in the water, feeling rather foolish.

"Now, I might be willin' to give ye the fish, if ye were to give me a boon."

A boon? Not a coin to her name. She thought everyone knew that. "I have nae coin to give ye," she told him, a little miffed that he'd expect her to pay for a fish that she could very well have caught on her own. Had he not been here distracting her, she would have caught more than enough by now. Ignoring him, she set about to do just that.

"I dinnae ask fer coin," he told her. "I asked fer a boon." He tossed the fish into her basket and waded back into the stream.

"Well, I do nae ken what ye expect me to give ye. I be as poor as a

3

field mouse." She bent over, cupped her hands, and waited for another fish to swim by. *Daft man.*

He was beside her again, laughing at her naiveté. "Well, I can think of somethin' ye can give me that will be more valuable than gold."

Onnleigh pursed her lips and shook her head dismissively. *What on earth do I have that anyone would think more valuable than gold? The man be tetched.* "I'll catch me own fish, thank ye verra kindly."

A moment later, he was tenderly taking her hands in his. Too stunned to utter a word, Onnleigh stood staring into Darwud MacCallen's dark brown eyes.

"Onnleigh, why do ye think I've been visitin' ye nearly every day?" he asked, his voice soft and low.

In truth, she couldn't rightly guess. No one ever came to visit her. "I dunnae," she whispered, curious, nervous and excited all at once.

He grinned, his lips a bit lopsided, before kissing the tips of her fingers. "I think I might like to marry ye, Onnleigh of Clan MacCallen."

Her heart bounced to her feet and back up again. *Marry? Me?* "Now I know ye're tetched," she told him dismissively. She'd given up the hope of ever having a husband or family of her own long ago. She and her da could barely afford to eat, let alone come up with any kind of dowry. Add those things to their less than stellar reputations, and, well, one could see how she would arrive at such a conclusion.

"Why would ye say that?" he asked, looking hurt.

Uncertainty settled in and she didn't rightly know how to answer the question.

"Ye be a beautiful lass, Onnleigh. Ye'd make any man proud to call ye wife."

'Twas laughable, wasn't it? Mayhap, just mayhap, the clan had forgotten all the rotten things her father had done to them. Mayhap they finally realized it was Grueber who had stolen their chickens, their vegetables, and anything else he could carry away with little effort. Mayhap they were ready to quit blaming her for his sins.

Oh, the possibilities were endless! For the first time in more than a decade, she felt *happy — nay, elated!*

Somehow she found her voice after swallowing hard twice. "Ye wish to marry me?"

"I might," he said playfully.

"I have no dowry, Darwud," she told him honestly. Her happy heart was beginning to pound against her breast.

"I do nae care about a dowry," he said, quite seriously. "'Tis ye I desire."

"Ye do?"

He nodded twice, his dark brown eyes twinkling in the afternoon sun.

"Ye dunnae jest?" she asked softly. Inner doubt was having an awful battle with her newfound hope and excitement.

"Nay, I dunnae jest. I want ye."

For the first time in her life, Onnleigh *ingen* Grueber of Clan MacCallen, felt beautiful, important, and special, all because of Darwud. Her excitement won out, beating down an inner voice that warned she should consider proceeding with a good deal of caution.

'Twas her first kiss, a wee bit awkward, but since she had nothing to compare it to, she thought it a most wonderful, sweet kiss. His lips felt warm against her own, her excitement building, soaring to never before experienced heights. Someone wanted her, Onnleigh, the thief's daughter. Darwud cared not about her father's reputation, cared not that she didn't have a dowry or a possession of her own to bring into the marriage. 'Twas her he wanted.

On her tiptoes, she clasped her hands behind his neck and kissed him back. *He wants to marry me. He thinks me bonny. He wants to marry me.*

One thing led to another, and before she knew what was happening, she was giving in to passions and desires she'd never felt before. Lying atop an old worn blanket on the rocky banks of the wide stream, Onnleigh became a woman in every sense of the word. It hadn't taken as long as she might have expected, but it didn't matter. Darwud MacCallen wanted to marry her.

He might just even love her.

# CHAPTER 1

$\mathcal{I}$n hindsight, Onnleigh should have listened to that inner voice. After she'd given herself completely to Darwud MacCallen, he kissed the tip of her nose, thanked her kindly and told her he'd be seeing her very soon.

For days afterward, she walked in the clouds, happily going about her daily routines with a song in her heart and a skip in her step. *Darwud wants to marry me.* What more could a girl such as she hope for in life?

Then a week passed by when she did not see him. She thought that quite odd, for he'd been coming to visit nearly every day for a month. Mayhap he had fallen ill or had been injured and that was what kept him away. After the tenth day, she had convinced herself of that very thing. "What kind of woman would I be if I did nae go to tend him? I'll be his wife soon and 'twill be me duty." She didn't want him to think she did not care about his health or well-being, so she set out for his home on a bright, clear morning.

She knew he still lived with his parents in a nice cottage near the clan keep. Darwud had oft spoke with a great deal of pride about the size of their home, the number of sheep they owned, and how well their crops did each year. Oh, she didn't quite believe everything he told her, but she didn't want to insult his male pride by sharing her skepticism.

It was not easy for her to take that long walk toward the keep. The last time she'd been inside the walls had been a most harrowing experience. She'd been but nine summers old and had made the mistake of listening to Thomas MacCallen. "Go ahead and take as many leeks as ye want, Onnleigh," he'd told her. "We ken ye're hungry. Maire's mum will nae care."

Well, Maire's mum *did* care. She cared so much in fact, that she took a switch to Onnleigh's backside and beat her all the way out of the garden, down the lane, and outside the walls. "Do nae ever come back here again, ye little thief!" she screamed as she tossed Onnleigh to the ground. That was how she got the scar that ran between her upper lip and her nose; she'd landed face first on a sharp rock, splitting her skin open in the process.

She had cried all the way home. Her da had been too into his cups to notice her tears or her cut lip.

She hadn't been back since.

With her head held high, her shoulders back, and a wee bit more pride than she had felt in an age—if ever—she crossed the frost-covered glen and headed down the path. She was wearing her best dress, which used to be her mum's, and tried to ignore the multiple patches. She had bathed, washed and combed her hair before working the wild auburn mane into a long braid. With her old shawl drawn tightly around her shoulders, she set off for Darwud's home.

Numerous neat and tidy cottages sat spread about the patch of land. Uncertain exactly which one was Darwud's, she walked until she came upon a woman in her garden.

"Excuse me," she said politely. "Can ye tell me which cottage be Darwud's?"

The woman stood from her half-frozen plants and eyed Onnleigh suspiciously. "Who are ye?" she asked before recognition set in. "Ye be Grueber's daughter." 'Twas a statement, not a question.

"Aye," she answered, her bravado starting to fade.

The woman shook her head in disgust. "His be the third house on the left," she motioned with her head. "But what do ye want him fer?"

It wasn't anyone's business, so she ignored the question, thanked her, and headed toward the cottage.

It was a quaint place, with a thatched roof and two stools that sat on either side of the door. She could smell stew cooking from within and her stomach rumbled. *I bet his mum be a right good cook*, she thought. Brushing down the skirt of her dress, she knocked on the door.

Moments later, a very pretty young woman answered. She had hair the color of spun gold and big green eyes. Her brow furrowed into a line of confusion when she saw Onnleigh standing on her doorstep. "Can I help ye?" she asked curiously.

Onnleigh offered her a curtsey. "I be here to see Darwud. Are ye his sister?"

The woman laughed. "Nay! I be his wife."

Onnleigh stood dumbfounded. "Darwud MacCallen's wife?" she managed to mumble.

"Aye, Darwud MacCallen's wife," the woman replied.

That inner voice began to scream, reminding Onnleigh just what a fool she was. Not wanting to cause a commotion, her mind raced for a way out of the situation. "Be he a short man, with red hair and a tic in one eye?"

The woman shook her head and rolled her eyes. "Nay. My Darwud be tall, with brown hair and brown eyes. I do no' ken another as ye described."

Her Darwud. Not Onnleigh's Darwud, but someone else's.

'Twas gut-wrenching news. She couldn't think, couldn't utter a word. Instead, she turned on her heels and left.

"Who are ye?" the young woman called out after her.

Not wanting to start any kind of commotion, she stopped, turned and smiled. "I be terrible sorry. 'Twas me mistake."

As soon as she was off the path she started running. But no matter how hard she pumped her legs, she could not escape the shame, the humiliation or her tears.

How could she be so stupid? So gullible?

He hadn't loved her. Of course, he hadn't said he had. But he said he wanted to marry her... No, he hadn't said that exactly. *I think I want to marry ye,* had been his exact words. She knew, because she had them burned into her memory.

'Twas all a lie. One big jest.

She stumbled twice, hurting both knees, the cold morning air burning her cheeks. By the time she reached her croft, her tear-streaked face was covered in sweat, her hair out of her braid, and her best dress had a new tear in it. Pushing past the fur that acted as a door, she saw her father lying on his bed, still sleeping off last night's drunk.

Swiping away tears, she looked around the space. Nothing more than one room with a dirt floor. Her father's bed sat against the wall to her right, her palette on the left. An ages-old, uneven table and two tree trunks for chairs sat in the middle, the firepit in front of it. The few pots she owned were stacked neatly on a shelf.

This was all she had ever known. This tiny hut, built into the side of a hill.

For a brief while, eleven days to be exact, she had dared to hope for more than this. Dared to believe that someone wanted her as wife. Allowed herself to believe the pretty words and kind gestures had been real.

Turning, she left the hut and headed to the small copse of trees behind it. 'Twas there, on her knees behind a fallen tree, that she let all the tears, frustration and anger out. Her grief came in great waves and wracking sobs.

She cursed Darwud to the devil, cursed men in general, as well as her own stupidity.

*How could anyone be so cruel?* How could a man lie like he had? Why? Why would he do such a thing?

A long while later, her tears shed but her shame still burning within, she took several deep breaths. The sun had burned away the morning frost, but not the dead, cold chill that lingered in her heart. She had searched and searched her mind and her heart for some memory of something awful she must have done at some point in her life. Some horrible, terrible act that would explain why she deserved to be used and thrown away. But she found nothing.

"Onnleigh!" her father's voice came booming through the trees. "Onnleigh!"

'Twould do no good to pretend she hadn't heard him. Wiping her tears on the hem of her dress, she took a deep breath and started back to the hut. She was halfway home when her father popped through a patch of overgrown brush. He glowered at her with bloodshot eyes. "Where the bloody hell have ye been?" he shouted harshly. "I been waitin' all day to eat!"

"I be sorry, Da," she told him half-heartedly, fully aware he'd been asleep all morn.

"Are ye tryin' to starve me to death?" he asked as she approached.

"Nay, Da," she said, standing on shaky legs. She was in no mood for one of his tirades. Her heart was shattered, but there'd be no sharing that with Grueber, for he could not have cared any less.

He stared at her as he yawned and scratched his belly with a dirty hand. "Well, quit standin' there and go fix me somethin' to eat!"

Oh, how she wished she had the courage to tell him to go fix his own bloody food! She rushed back to the croft and set about making him a fish soup. *Fish.* Blasted, ugly fish. When she lopped off the head of the trout, she imagined 'twas Darwud's head staring back at her.

Mayhap the problem didn't lie with her, but with Darwud. Mayhap he was nothing but a lying, flea-infested cur and coward.

She decided he was not worth shedding more tears over. Still, she did not feel any better. No one had loved her, not since her mum died. 'Twas the plain and simple truth. Though why it was impossible for anyone to care for her, she didn't know. Her da didn't love anyone or anything other than his brew. Her clanspeople, the people she should have been able to trust and go to in an hour of need, couldn't abide the sight of her, let alone find a shred of love or decency in their hearts. She was nothing more than the daughter of a thief, layabout and drunkard. She would never be anything more than that to anyone. Not ever.

'Twas a painful thing to realize, to try to live with. But what could she do? Not a bloody thing.

There would be no husband, no nice cottage with rushes to cover the floors, or flowers or gardens to plant. No children to love or tend to. No rich stews or sweet cakes to make for them. No friends and family who would come to visit.

There was nothing but the hovel she shared with her drunken father. Two old dresses, a pair of boots with holes in the toes, and naught else.

The tears returned, but not with the same vengeance as before. They were melancholy tears. Tears shed out of the deep sorrow of realizing, with finality, that there would be nothing else for her in this life but what she already had.

THE DAY after she managed the courage to go to the keep, Darwud MacCallen showed up on her doorstep.

And he was angry.

"Why did ye go to me cottage?" he demanded as he pulled her out of the croft by the arm. His grip was tight, his fingers digging into her tender flesh.

Onnleigh didn't think he had the right to be angry with her. She hadn't lied to *him*. She hadn't been the one to whisper false words into *his* ears. "Why? Did I upset yer *wife?*"

He continued to pull her away from the croft. "Ye fool! Ye had no right to do that! To go to me home!"

She yanked her arm out of his grasp and stopped in her tracks. "No right?"

"No right!"

"Pardon me, but nearly a fortnight ago, ye told me ye thought ye might like to marry me. Ye were all sweet and filled with pretty words. Words I was stupid enough to believe," she all but spat at him.

"'Twas nae me fault ye believed them," he said through gritted teeth. His face was red with anger, his hands drawn into tight fists.

"Ye're right, 'twas *me own* fault."

He took a step closer. "Do nae ever come to me home again, do ye hear me?"

"I would nae wan' anywhere near yer home." Her voice was filled with anger.

She could almost see his mind racing for his next words.

"Does yer wife ken what a liar and cheat ye are?"

In hindsight, 'twas not the right question to ask. His arm swung out, and he struck her across the cheek with the back of his hand, sending her to the hard earth. Her head swam; her stomach lurched with an ugly blend of fear and anger. The metallic taste of blood filled her mouth as her cheek throbbed in time with her frightened heart.

He stood over her, hands on his hips, warning her in a harsh and angry voice. "If ye ever tell another soul what we did, I'll deny it. No one will believe ye. Everyone kens ye're a liar and a thief, just like yer da."

His words struck deep and cruelly. "And if I carry yer child? What then, Darwud?"

'Twas the second least intelligent thing she could have said that day. In a fury, he pulled her to her feet by her hair, only to slap her again. That second brutal smack was much worse than the first. She fell to the ground again, this time sprawled out on her back. White dots of pain floated in her eyes.

"Ye really are a stupid whore. Do ye honestly think anyone will believe ye over me?"

'Twas his laughter, which came after, that hurt more than his words or his calloused hands. He was laughing at her, comfortable with the knowledge that he was right. No one would believe her.

He left her there with her pulse pounding in dread, her head swimming, her heart shattering into tiny slivers.

All because she was Grueber's daughter.

# CHAPTER 2

## ONE YEAR LATER

onnor MacCallen looked out the small, narrow window of his private study at the beauty of his lands: rolling hills covered in green-brown grass which had yet to see a touch of winter snow, lay dormant and quiet. Not far from the keep was a small hill, a bump really in comparison to the larger, grander hills that lay beyond. There, just outside the gardens, at the top of that bump, stood three wych elms. During the warmer months, mothers did their sewing as they sat on bright blankets watching bairns play at their feet, or keeping an eye on the older children as they chased one another. Now, the space sat empty. But he knew that, come spring, the hill would be filled once again with mothers, babes, and weans.

On the west side of the keep, his men were training for battle. He could not see them, but he could hear the distinct sound of metal clanking against metal, commanders shouting at the younger men—their grunts, curses and laughter.

Inside the keep, his people were excitedly preparing for the upcoming Yuletide. Evergreens and holly were hung in nearly every room, special foods were being prepared, and soon, he and his brothers would carve a special log to be burned on Yuletide eve.

No matter the time of year, these lands were paradise, heaven on earth, no others more beautiful or more serene.

'Twas also the most lonely of places.

With arms crossed over his broad chest, Connor leaned his blonde head against the sill as he continued to stare at his lands with a heavy, melancholy heart.

These tranquil moments would not last long if he could not broker a peace accord with the Randalls. How long their clans had been at war was anyone's guess. Decade after decade of warring for a reason or reasons no one could remember. Now 'twas up to him to find a way to end it.

"Are ye ready?"

The question, he was certain, had little to do with where his mind had been.

He needn't look to see who was standing behind him. 'Twas his grandminny, Bruanna, a woman as old as dirt.

With a heavy sigh, he turned away from the window. "For what?"

When she furrowed her brow as she was now doing, it deepened the lines of age that creased a once quite beautiful face. Light from the candles that were scattered here and there, glanced off her pewter hair. Tapping her walking stick once against the stone floor, she said, "To go to the wishin' well, ye daft boy!"

*God's bones, be it that time already?*

"I cannae take ye this time. Ask Braigh," he told her.

She cracked the stick against the floor again, this time a wee bit more forcefully than last. "I will nae ask Braigh!"

"Grandminny, I have too much to do this day."

She'd not give in. "Ye ken why," she reminded him. "Ye and I *must* go today."

He let loose a breath of frustration. They'd been taking the same trek almost every year for the past 28 of his life—minus the four he spent fostering with the MacKinnons. A trek that took nearly half a day now, because she refused to ride a horse or be carried by wagon, and insisted they walk. "Grandminny—"

She cut off his protest. "Do nae tell me how busy ye be. I ken ye be chief and I ken what it involves. I be no' some dimwitted auld woman who cannae even chew her own food or does nae ken the day of the week. We must leave now or we'll miss the time."

Every year was the same. Every year, on the anniversary of his grandfather's birth, they would go to the wishing well to make special wishes. They had to be at that blasted wishing well before the four o'clock hour *elst the wish will nae come true,* or so Bruanna believed. Connor didn't give much credence to wishes or fairies or any of the other things his Grandminny believed in.

He tried again to reason with her. His words fell on deaf ears.

"We must go today," she told him, undeterred. "This may verra well be me last chance."

'Twas the same ploy she'd been using for the last seven years. *I be gettin' on in years. I dunnae ken how many more days I have left.*

Years of experience with the woman who had helped raise him, who had outlived all of her own children—and rumor had it was there when Christ was born—told him arguing was futile.

"Verra well," he said with a measure of resignation. Arguing with Bruanna was as pointless as trying to move a mountain of dirt with one hand. "But let us nae tarry long, fer I *do* have important work."

Her frown evaporated instantly, replaced with a smile that showed three missing bottom teeth. "Thank ye, grandson. Have I ever told ye that ye be me favorite?"

Taking her gently by the elbow, he smiled. "All the time, unless I have vexed ye, for then Braigh and Ronald are yer favorites."

Her reply was nothing more than a happy cackle that filled the hallway.

THEY COULD HAVE REACHED the well in an hour, were Bruanna willing to ride. Because she refused to sit atop a horse unless God Himself came down from the heavens and told her to, she and Connor walked —or rather, Connor walked and she shuffled along at a snail's pace— on the three-hour journey to the wishing well.

As his grandminny prattled on about years gone by, Connor kept a watchful eye out for anyone who might intend to do them harm. The only thing he and his neighboring clans could agree upon was that the old wishing well was neutral and sacred ground. None could fight there, nor kill, nor war against one another on that tiny spot of land. Still, there was much ground to cover between his lands and that blasted old well that many people, including Bruanna, believed held magical powers.

Half tempted to pick the woman up and carry her the rest of the way, Connor continued to scan the horizon. Though the well and a small patch of ground that surrounded it was sacred, the earth on which they currently trod was not. Therefore he had made certain to have two-dozen mounted men spread out in all directions to help maintain a watchful eye.

Located near the base of the mountain in a wide, deep valley, the well had sat for centuries. Remnants of an old fortress, built by Norseman who had come from afar to claim the land as their own, lay scattered around the well. He put no faith in that old well. Connor chose to pray to the one true God instead of looking into old wells for answers.

After several brief stops along the way, to allow his grandminny to rest, they finally reached their destination. The air here was considerably warmer, the valley and surrounding mountains acting as a bowl to keep the warm air in. Still, there was a nice breeze and a bright blue sky dotted with fluffy clouds that leant beauty to the place.

There sat the well, the object of his consternation for the past ten years.

Built with granite, lined with pitch, it sat near the wide stream the Norse had dammed for a time before the Scots won out. Now the stream flowed freely to the points God had intended.

Many years ago, when the land had been declared sacred, someone had laid large rocks around the well, to signify the agreed upon boundaries. A wide circle, some one hundred feet in circumference. Outside that boundary 'twas an every-man-for-himself existence. But inside? Many a man had jumped the rocks to claim sanctuary to keep from being killed by an enemy, a marauder, or an angry father against a man who had done his daughter wrong.

Trees had grown up through the old stone walls, through the last part of the roof of the long old building. Brush and scrabble that none dared touch grew wherever it wished. 'Twas as deserted a place as ever there was.

"There it be!" Bruanna exclaimed happily.

Connor rolled his eyes. "Did ye think it had moved?" he asked sarcastically.

His grandminny whacked him on the arm with her walking stick. "Don't be blasphemous!" she scolded him.

*Blasphemous?* He didn't have the mental fortitude to argue the point that to put more faith in a well than in God was to blaspheme. He kept his thoughts to himself.

Bruanna shuffled in hurried fashion toward the well, carefully stepping over the rocks. Connor hurried as well, but not with the same enthusiasm. He simply wanted to get this annual sojourn over with so he could return home to important business.

"Do ye remember what it says?" she asked him as she looked in awe at the great stone lid that sat against the wall of the well, facing east.

How could he forget? He'd only had the blasted runes burned into his memory since he was old enough to recite it. Loving his grandminny as he did, he recited the words to her. *"May your journey be quiet and your days of joy long. May your deeds remain strong for Odin. May your love stay true to your noble heart."*

Her eyes gleamed with pride. "Aye, laddie, ye have the way of it."

How anyone could put so much stock into a pile of stones and words carved into a lid, he did not know. Especially when it had such a dark history surrounding it.

Connor thought it all nonsense, of course. His faith did not lie in wishes and enchanted wells. People made wishes at other times of the year, though what or who granted those he didn't know and daren't ask his grandmother.

Still, he supposed if it gave her some measure of peace and happiness, who was he to try to take that away? Pushing his frustration aside, he decided he should probably enjoy this moment with his dear grandmother. This was her seventieth summer on earth and though he believed she'd outlive him and the rest of his clan, there was a distinct possibility she was not as immortal as either he or she believed.

"Do ye remember how to make yer wish?" he asked as he stood beside her.

She quirked a brow. "Of course I remember, ye heathen!" she said playfully.

Reaching into his sporran, he pulled out a small coin and tried handing it to her.

"Nay, lad, no coin today," she told him. "If I want this wish to come true, I must use somethin' more valuable to me than coin. We must make our wish today, and by Christmastide, we will know if it has come to pass or no'."

'Twas her belief that the most important and special of wishes required her to give up something she treasured, to show her deep sincerity. Connor smiled at her. "And what will ye be usin' this year?"

Reaching into her pouch with gnarled fingers, she pulled out something he could not see and held it tightly in her hands. "What will *ye* be usin'?" she asked him.

"I fear I only brought coin today."

Instead of chastising him for forgetting protocols of years passed, she smiled up at him. 'Twas as loving and tender a smile as any grand-minny could have for a favored grandson. "Then we shall use this and make our wish together."

Playfully, he asked, "and what if my wish comes true and yours does nae?"

"Who says we'll nae be wishin' fer the same thing?"

He had no wish prepared. Oh, there were things he longed for, things he prayed to God for on a daily basis, but he hadn't come to the well with a particular wish in mind.

"I ken what it is yer heart desires, grandson," she told him with a most serious tone and expression.

"Ye do?"

"Aye," she nodded. "Ye wish fer a lovin' wife, children, and peace."

With a raised brow and pursed lips, he asked, "How do ye ken this?"

She cackled and patted his arm. "Och, laddie, ye've been longin' fer these things since before ye had a beard to shave."

He hadn't thought his heart was so transparent.

"'Tis true, is it nae?" she asked.

He took in a deep breath. "Aye, it be true. I pray each day fer a wife and bairns and fer peace fer our clan."

He'd had a wife once and a bairn. But Maire had died within hours of giving birth to their son. Born far too early, the wee babe they'd named William, after Connor's father, died the following day. That was more than four years ago. He thought he'd never get over the loss. But now? Now he was chief of Clan MacCallen and it was important —for himself and the clan—that he try again. He was a very lonely man.

"Then we shall wish fer the same thing this day, lad," Bruanna took his hand in hers and gave it a gentle squeeze. "I shall count to three before tossing this into the well and we shall wish together for all that ye truly want in this life."

*All me heart desires?*

Though it went against everything he believed in, Connor MacCallen decided that one little wish could not hurt.

BRAIGH HAD SEEN the lass crouched low behind the ancient, crumbling wall. She was hard to miss, with her auburn hair shining in the afternoon sun. He'd quietly drawn his sword and watched with a careful eye. 'Twas sacred ground his brother and grandmother were on, as well as the lass with the fiery hair. Still, one could not be too careful. The enemy could come in any form.

From atop his horse, with sword ready, he was too far away to hear the conversation taking place between Connor and Bruanna, but close enough that he could intervene if necessary.

At the lass's feet was a woven basket filled with something he could not see. Weapons perhaps? Nay, he doubted it.

The longer he stared, the more he thought he recognized her. Some vague memory from his past began to creep into his mind. But no matter how hard he tried to pull it forth, it escaped him.

Plenty of women in his clan had been blessed with red hair, even his own wife. But this girl's hair? It blazed red and auburn and brown. Her build was slight and small. Young she was, mayhap no more than five and ten, he reckoned. She wore an odd dress, at least as far as he could tell, that looked old and worn. He could just make out patches on the sleeves as well as one large patch on the side of the skirt.

He turned to watch his grandmother and older brother's annual tradition of tossing something into the well. Though he couldn't hear them, he was quite sure he knew what they were saying. Connor was undoubtedly holding his tongue, daring not to speak his true thoughts as they pertained to the well. His grandminny was more likely than not doing her best to convince him to open his mind and heart to the possibility that it might just work this time.

Braigh believed in the power of the well, even if his brother didn't. It was his fervent belief that his wife, Lorna, would never have fallen in love with him were it not for the wish he made here less than a year ago. He'd wished for *her* in particular, with all that he had, for he had loved her since he first laid eyes on her when he was a lad. And now they were married and expecting their first babe in the spring.

Connor held Bruanna's hand as she tossed the coin or whatever she was offering up this year into the well. Long moments passed before they stepped away to begin the journey home. Braigh remained behind, watching the fiery-haired lass to make certain she would not pounce the moment his brother and grandminny stepped off the sacred ground.

The minutes stretched on and the girl made no attempt to move or attack. Feeling certain she was no foe, he tapped the flanks of his horse and left to follow his family home.

~

ONNLEIGH'S HEART pounded against her breast as she crouched behind the stone wall. She'd heard the horses coming before she'd seen them. Not knowing who approached, she ducked down and hid. Moments passed before she heard an auld woman's voice.

She hid for many reasons. Mostly because she was Grueber's daughter and did not want anyone to accuse her of trying to steal the coins from the well. She knew it couldn't be done, taking the coins, unless one lowered themselves into the well with a rope. And she only understood that because her da had tried before, unsuccessfully, and moaned about his misfortune for days after.

Still, she didn't wish to take the chance.

At first, she did not know who it was who had come to make their wish, but it didn't take long to figure it out. 'Twas Connor MacCallen and his grandminny.

She hadn't seen Connor in over a decade. Of all the children of her clan, he was one of the very few who had ever shown her a moment of kindness. But then he'd been sent away to foster somewhere, and she was left without a friend or ally to her name. Not long after, she'd been ostracized.

Straining her ears, she could hear him and Bruanna talking about their wishes. Only minutes before, Onnleigh had made a wish of her own. Though she didn't have a coin to her name, she had used the only thing of value she owned: a necklace. 'Twas worth nothing to anyone but her. 'Twas the only thing of her mum's she had left now, besides the clothes she was wearing. A long strand of leather with one tiny pink shell affixed to it. Not knowing if the wish would work without a coin, she was mighty glad when she heard Bruanna say, *If I want this wish to come true, I must use somethin' more valuable to me than coin.* Mayhap there was a chance her wish might come true after all.

When Onnleigh heard Connor admit to wanting a wife and child, it nearly stole her breath away.

After they left, she lowered herself so her back was against the ancient, decrepit wall. Tears streamed down her cheeks as she lifted her sleeping babe from the basket and held her close.

A beautiful little girl named Nola, born at the end of August, with little wisps of red hair and big blue eyes. Nothing of the man who sired her was visible in the wee babe's face. For that, she was mightily grateful.

There had been no yarn to weave blankets, no soft linens with which to make clothes for her daughter. So she had taken her one and only chemise and fashioned several gowns for her daughter out of it. She had cut an old blanket into squares for nappies.

When she had discovered she was carrying Darwud's babe, she thought her world had come to an end. Out of fear, she hadn't shared her discovery with her da. Hiding her growing belly had been difficult, but not impossible, for he was too wrapped up in his own miserable life to pay any attention to hers.

On a warm summer's night in May, Grueber died in his sleep. Onnleigh shed no tears over the loss, for what was she truly missing? He had never provided for her, had been demanding, mean-spirited and drunk every day she could remember.

Nay, she had no tears to waste for the man who had sired her but never cared one whit about her.

So she dug a hole far from their hut, wrapped him in his filthy sheet, and rolled him down the hill and into his final resting spot. It hadn't been easy, but why should she expect such when he'd been nothing but difficult in life?

Naught much changed after his death, for he hadn't been any help to her while living. Admittedly, things were far more peaceful after he was gone. So much so that she quit dreading the thought of impending motherhood and chose to focus instead on what joy a babe of her own might bring.

A child she could love and cherish, who would love her back. She'd be a patient and kind mother, would give the babe everything in this world she possibly could.

It mattered not that Darwud had sired Nola, or that he didn't even know of her existence. Nay, the only thing that mattered was all the love Onnleigh had in her heart to give another being. Suddenly, she didn't feel quite so alone in this world.

Then reality set in, just minutes after giving birth.

She hadn't a clue what she was doing. She'd never been around a babe before, at least not that she could remember. There was no one to turn to for advice or help. The only things she knew with a certainty were how to love her, feed her and keep her clean.

It had taken days for her milk to come in. She worried her poor Nola would end up starving to death. Blessedly, that did not happen, but still she worried.

The babe seemed to be hungry all the time. Day and night. Onnleigh worried her milk might not be good enough for the babe, didn't know how soon before she should try giving her little bits of food, such as gruel. Did all babes eat this much?

Were all babes as beautiful as hers? Did they cry like she did? Did they pee as often as she did? Was she too cold? Too hot?

Endless questions and no answers.

Weeks passed and Nola grew, but Onnleigh worried it was not by enough. Many a night, she walked the floors, cradling a crying babe and not knowing what on earth she should do for her.

After a time, Onnleigh's confidence in her abilities to provide for this beautiful, sweet babe began to wane. She finally realized she could not do it. Could not give her anything, not even a decent gown to call her own. They had nothing in this world but each other. Soon, she began to realize that love mayhap was not enough.

She'd tried praying, as she remembered her mum had done before she died. But prayer wasn't working. Her heart grew heavier with each passing day.

With nothing left to do, Onnleigh bundled up her babe and headed to the wishing well. She could remember going there as a little girl, with her mother, to make wishes she could not recall. The well was not far from her croft, and thankfully, Nola slept on the trek through the woods and over the rise.

Onnleigh had made her wish.

And only moments later, Connor MacCallen had appeared almost out of nowhere, with his grandminny. Together, she'd heard them make a wish for him. *A wife, children, and peace.*

She couldn't give him a wife, and peace was just as impossible.

But she could give him one thing. Something she loved more than her next breath, something she did not in truth want to part with, but she knew there was no other way.

# CHAPTER 3

'Twas long after the evening meal when Connor made his way to the tiny kirk that stood east of the keep. Made of stone, with tall, narrow windows, the kirk had been built by his great, great grandsire.

Just as he had done every day since losing his wife and son, he waited until long after everyone was asleep before he set out. Stepping inside the cold night air of the kirk, he lit a candle from one of the torches that lined the entrance and made his way to the front. There he set the candle on the stone bench and knelt before the large wooden cross.

His prayers rarely differed from one night to the next. As always, he prayed for peace for his clan and for a wife who would love him and give him many children. Tonight, he added an extra prayer for his grandminny, that God would see fit to give him a few more years with her.

With eyes closed and hands folded together, so focused was he in his prayer, he hadn't heard anyone enter the kirk. Much time passed before he was finished. Making the sign of the cross, he left the bench.

As he made his way down the aisle toward the door, he noticed something out of the corner of his eye; something he knew with a certainty had not been there when he arrived.

There, on the last pew, was a basket.

When he held the candle closer to see what was inside, his eyes nearly bulged from their sockets.

A wee sleeping babe with little tufts of red hair lay bundled in an old worn blanket inside that basket. He blinked once, then twice, in case he wasn't seeing clearly. But aye, he was. Quickly, he scanned the inside of the kirk for any sign of another person. There was none other than he and the babe.

For the longest time he sat next to the basket in hopes that someone had simply set it down for a short while, mayhap to use the privy, or whatever else would necessitate leaving a babe there unattended.

An hour passed and no one had come to claim the babe. All the while, he tried to convince himself that the babe had not been abandoned. But in his heart, he knew it had been.

BY THE TIME MORNING DAWNED, the entire keep was in an uproar over the babe someone had abandoned in the kirk.

Some believed 'twas God's handiwork, that he had placed the babe there for Connor to rescue.

Others believed 'twas an abomination, either the fact a mother had left her child, or the child itself. "A mum would nae leave a perfectly healthy babe." "The babe must be possessed to make her mum leave her like that."

Connor had a different way of thinking. More likely than not, the child's parents had abandoned her in the kirk in hopes that the priest would find her a good home. It had to be someone from within his own clan, for the gates were locked and guarded each night.

"Ye cannae be serious," his mother-in-law Helen scoffed at that idea.

"Aye, I am quite serious."

"But ye cannae do that, Connor! Ye cannae claim the child as yer own!"

They were standing in his private study, having yet another battle. There had been many betwixt them over the years. For some reason, Helen held the belief that he actually cared what she thought. He didn't. Never had. Not when he had returned from fostering, not when he had stolen her daughter away in the middle of the night to marry her, and definitely not now. He was trying to be polite, but she didn't make it easy. Helen was a hard woman. Hard to figure out. Hard to get along with. Hard to like. Still, he felt he owed it to his dead wife to be as kind as he was able to her mum.

"But if you and Margaret get married and have babes of yer own —" she began.

Had he not been cradling his daughter in his arms, he would have shouted. "I am *nae* going to marry Margaret."

She scoffed again. "Bah! I've seen how ye look at her with lust in yer eyes. Ye ken ye want to marry her, but ye refuse because ye ken I want ye to."

*I stare at her all right, but because I find it difficult to believe she was Maire's sister.* "I do nae stare at her with lust." In truth, he tried to avoid her at all costs.

"Ye only say these things because ye dunnae like me," she said dismissively. "Either way, if ye claim this child, when ye do marry someday, 'twill be a bastard child who inherits instead of yer own blood."

The woman had a gift of saying the wrong things at the worst of times. "Helen," he said as he held the babe to his chest. "Ye may leave now."

"This will break Margaret's heart," she told him, her voice harsh.

*I was nae aware she possessed one.* "Good day," he said.

Connor let loose a long breath of relief when she slammed the door behind her.

"That, lass, is a woman ye should never model yerself after. She be cold, with a heart of lead, that one," he told the bundle in his arms. She was a sweet babe, with bright, dark blue eyes.

28

Thankfully, his cook, Louisa, stood behind his decision. She'd even gone so far as to acquire goat's milk and a wee flagon with which the child could suckle. "Nae near as good as mother's milk, but 'twill do," Louisa had told him just an hour before.

Now the babe was happy and content, looking up at him as she sucked on her little fist.

While he would love to claim this child, he sincerely hoped the mother would change her mind and come for her daughter. 'Twasn't that he didn't want the babe. On the contrary, a little part of him wished the mother *wouldn't* change her mind so he could keep her. He hoped 'twas desperation that had forced the mother to give up her child. But he could not think of one person amongst his people who was that desperate. His clan had been blessed for many years with fertile soil and abundant crops. He doubted 'twas poverty that motivated such an act. Nay, it had to be something else.

Just whom the babe belonged to was a mystery, so he'd sent his brothers, Braigh and Ronald out to question their people, to see if anyone was missing a bairn or had recently birthed one.

In the meantime, he would take this wee cherub as his own. Mayhap God was finally answering his prayers. Granted, not in a typical fashion, with a wife first, and children second. Still, the Lord worked in mysterious ways, did He not?

Besides, he rather enjoyed the look of stunned horror on Helen's face when he told her he was going to declare the child his if the mother did not return in a fortnight. 'Twas probably not the most Christian thing to do. He'd ask God's forgiveness later that night.

LEAVING her daughter in the kirk had been the single most difficult thing Onnleigh had ever done. She'd barely gotten out the door when the tears began to fall. But she told herself she had to wait until she was beyond the walls, out of earshot of the guards or anyone else who might be awake at that hour, before she could let it all out.

The decision to give Nola away had not been easy. It left her bereft and empty, as if her heart had been torn from her chest and left out in the sun to wither.

Sleep did not come easily; her breasts began to ache with a need to feed the child, her arms and heart ached with a need to hold her. By morning, her bed was soaked with tears and spent milk.

Brokenhearted, cloaked in guilt, she tried to go about her daily routine, but 'twas next to impossible. For weeks, she had carried Nola with her wherever she went. To collect eggs, milk the cow, gather berries—her babe was always there, tied to her chest in a sling made from an old sheet.

She slept with the sling clutched to her chest, wept openly and without restraint.

Her arms were empty, but not nearly as empty as her heart.

For two days, she questioned her decision. What if Connor did not want a cast-off? What if they could not find a home for her? Worse yet, what if they gave her to someone who wouldn't or couldn't love her as much as Onnleigh? Those were the things that kept her awake at night.

By the end of the second day, her breasts were so engorged she could barely walk. She tried to press the milk out with her hands, but the relief was short-lived. Her breasts screamed for her babe. Her heart ached with longing to hold Nola in her arms once more.

Back and forth she argued in her mind. *I did it fer her. Ye cannae take care o' her, have nothin' to offer. She deserves more than ye can give her.* But her heart? Her heart worried that whomever was kind enough to take her in, would do it for the wrong reasons. Mayhap they'd only take her to use as a servant and not a child they loved? What if they could not protect her in the future, especially from men like Darwud?

The guilt at having given up the one thing she'd ever truly loved in her life was overwhelming. The tears would not stop; the ache in her heart would not subside. 'Twas unbearable.

By dawn on the third day, she realized she couldn't do it, couldn't go on without Nola. If she could just see her, find out if Connor had taken her in or given her to someone else, she'd feel better, could then move on. There was nothing left for her here, save for a few chickens and the milk cow. No fond or happy memories, save for those few, too-short memories of her daughter.

Nay, she would go to the keep, learn what she could about what had become of the babe.

If Connor had taken her in to raise as his own, then Onnleigh would move on. Mayhap another clan would take Onnleigh, offer her a new home, a new chance at a future. She didn't want to go to the Randalls, for they were the enemy. But somewhere beyond MacCallen lands there had to be a place where no one knew she was Grueber's daughter. A place where she wouldn't be looked down upon simply because of the thief who had sired her. A place with kind people who would open their arms to her.

Certainly, somewhere on God's earth, such a place must exist.

She had draped her shawl over her head to disguise herself. The only other dress she owned was wrapped inside a small bundle, along with some wild berries and a hunk of cheese. The gates were open this morn, to allow the people who lived just outside the walls to enter freely, to do business, seek an audience with the chief, or visit with family and friends.

Onnleigh kept her head down, but her eyes and ears open in the hope she might hear some news about her babe. She wound her way through the crowds, silently listening, hoping, praying she could learn where Nola was. Her breasts ached, no matter how tightly she bound them with the old sheet. As she walked, she could feel her milk slowly leaking down her breasts and into the waist of her skirt. Hopefully, no one would notice.

She meandered out of doors for the longest time, but thus far, no one was speaking about the abandoned child. Fear crept into her heart with the thought that perhaps Connor hadn't seen the basket when he left the kirk that night. What if he hadn't, and Nola had succumbed to the elements? Fearing the worst, she made her way to the kirk. No basket, no babe.

Mayhap if she could not find answers without, she could find them within. Drawing on courage she hadn't realized she possessed, she made her way back around the keep and into the kitchens.

She took a few steps inside, allowing her eyes to adjust, grateful for the warmth that surrounded her. A tall woman of mayhap fifty stood at a table chopping vegetables. Brown hair just beginning to gray at the edges, encircled her round face. Onnleigh did not recognize her and prayed the woman would not know her either. Other people, men and women, were busy scrambling about the large space, lost in their own thoughts or concentrating on their chores.

The woman tossed the vegetables into a large wooden bowl and headed toward the hearth, where a large pot was simmering. When she caught sight of Onnleigh, she stood to her full height. "Who be ye and what do ye want?"

Frozen in place, she had to think quickly. She couldn't very well say she was here to retrieve the babe she had abandoned three days ago. "I've come to see if ye have work."

The woman rolled her eyes as she scraped the vegetables into the pot with the edge of a long knife. "Well, there be plenty of work to do around here, but none I can give ye. Keepin' us busy, night and day, she is. 'Tis nae fair nor just, but none will listen to me."

Just who *she* was, Onnleigh didn't know and had not the courage to ask. "I be terrible sorry to have bothered ye," she said.

"If ye can find the chief, ye might ask him if he's willin' to pry apart that auld hag's tight fists and give ye a place, but I would nae hold me breath were I ye."

The chief? Nay, she'd rather be stripped naked, her body slathered in honey, and thrown on an ant hill than go see him. William MacCallen had terrified her when she was a child. He'd been the biggest man she'd ever seen and the scar that ran across his cheek did nothing to soften his hard looks, his broken nose, and those deep, penetrating eyes.

Thanking the woman, she curtsied and left the kitchen, and walked across the little courtyard to the keep. The door creaked ever so slightly when she pulled it open. She'd never set foot inside before, and had no idea where, if at all, she should look for her daughter.

The entryway was tall and narrow, with three doorways branching off. She decided to continue straight ahead, which led her to a large gathering room. Trestle tables had been pulled away and put against the wall to allow maids to sweep old rushes and spread new. Two young women were standing near a long sideboard, polishing pewter mugs. One looked up, offered her a smile before returning to her work.

Ahead, and off to her left, was a staircase leading up to the second floor. The gathering room was open to the halls above on three sides. Not knowing what else to do, she decided to take the stairs.

No one paid her any mind as she ascended to the second floor and walked the cramped hallways. She dared not open any closed doors, or even knock, lest she be found out. Instead, she walked along at a slow pace and listened, peeking only into those rooms with open doors.

At the end of the hallway on her left, a heavy wooden door stood slightly ajar. Just steps away, her heartbeat escalated when she heard her daughter whimpering. At the sweet, merciful sound, her breasts swelled painfully as more milk began to leak.

A quick glance up and down the hallway told her she was alone. Slowly, ever so slowly, she pushed the door open. Pulling her shawl away from her face, she was able to see 'twas a nice sized bedchamber, with a tall, four-poster bed set in the center. Two trunks sat under the window on the wall straight ahead. To her left was an empty fireplace.

At the foot of the bed, sitting on a heavy trunk, was the basket containing her daughter. She rushed to her, dropped the bundle at her feet, scooped Nola into her arms, and held her close. "Wheesht, babe, I be here now."

Nola's whimpers increased, as did the ache in Onnleigh's breast. Shutting the door, she looked for a safe spot to feed her. To her right, opposite the bed, was a darkened doorway. Onnleigh took a few tentative steps forward before she noticed a light coming from within.

'Twas a small room, with two narrow windows that faced east, just like the room she'd just left. There she found a cradle, a trunk, and a padded chair. Turning the chair away from the doorway, she quickly sat, untied her tunic, and began to nurse her babe.

Nola sucked greedily, covering her ear with one tiny fist, just as she had done almost since the day she'd been born. The relief at seeing her daughter safe was undeniable. Onnleigh's breasts felt much the same way as her heart.

As Nola fed, Onnleigh inspected her closely. She was wearing a very fine little gown of soft ivory linen. Little woolens covered her legs, a bonnet her head. The blanket was finely woven in shades of creams and yellows.

*I could never have given ye such things,* she thought guiltily. *Ye deserve things like these, my sweet Nola.*

As the babe finished one breast, Onnleigh switched her to the other. The moments passed by, and Onnleigh began to have second thoughts. Pretty gowns, warm blankets and woolens, a cradle. She could never have given her child any of those things. Was she being selfish by wanting to take Nola away, to keep her all to herself? *Aye, I am.*

Nola finished eating and fell asleep. Onnleigh sat in the quiet, tiny room for a while longer, whispering promises. "I cannae give ye much, Nola. All I can give ye is me love, and I fear that be nae enough. Love will nae keep ye warm in winter or yer stomach full, or clothes on yer back. But I can give ye to someone who will give ye all those things. I pray, babe, that he will also be able to love ye as if ye were his own."

With her mind made up again, she laid Nola on her lap whilst she retied the laces of her tunic. A cold chill filled her heart, bringing with it gooseflesh. Pulling her shawl around, she lifted her babe and held her close to her heart.

With tears in her eyes, she knew she had to say goodbye now, not look back, not ever question her decision to do what was best for her child.

～

"WHAT ARE YE DOIN' with me daughter?"

Terror rippled up and down Onnleigh's spine at the sound of Connor's voice. She recognized it from the wishing well. Gone was the playfulness he'd shared with his grandminny. Now he sounded quite angry. Her mind raced for a way out.

Slowly, she stood and turned. Och! He had grown into a handsome devil of a man. She had not been able to see him that day at the well, only heard his voice.

His blonde hair fell past his shoulders; his bright green eyes were penetrating. He wore a dark blue tunic with leather laces, the sleeves rolled up to his elbows. His trews were pulled taut over hard thighs, his leather boots strapped around thick calves. It took only a moment to realize he could snap her like a twig.

Stammering, she answered as honestly as she could. "I, I heard her cry, m'laird, so I picked her up and held her. She be asleep now, see?" Taking a few steps forward on very shaky legs, she held Nola up for his inspection.

"She was alone?" he asked with a quirked brow.

"Aye, m'laird," she answered softly as the worry and dread continued to grow.

She could see he was sizing her up, looking for any sign of deceit. A long, awkward silence passed between them.

"Who are ye?"

That was a question she did not wish to answer. "I'll be leavin' now, m'laird. Would ye like yer babe back?"

Slowly, he shook his head nay. "I asked who ye are."

Clearing her throat in an attempt to dislodge the knot, she finally answered. "Onnleigh."

A flicker of something flashed in those bright green eyes of his. "Onnleigh, who?"

Another question she did not wish to answer. But because he was blocking the doorway, she saw no way around it. "Onnleigh *ingen* Grueber."

There it 'twas, that flicker of recognition before he pulled his shoulders back. Her hands began to shake as she braced herself for the insults that were sure to follow before he began to search for signs that she'd stolen something. Ingen Grueber was synonymous with *the thief's daughter*. 'Twould never change.

"I be sorry to have bothered ye, m'laird," she told him. Still he did not move.

"Why are ye here?"

She hated lying above all things. But there was no choice in the matter—for her honesty would most assuredly get her stoned out of the keep—so she lied. "I came lookin' fer work."

"As what?"

"Scullery maid, but the nice woman in the kitchen said there was no work to be had, so I will be on me way now." Once again, she tried handing Nola to him, but he made no attempt to take her.

"Did ye nae think to ask *me* if there was work?"

She shook her head, slightly confused with his question. "Nae, m'laird. The lady in the kitchen said to seek out the chief, but I be certain he be far too busy fer the likes o' me."

"I am never too busy to help one of our own who is in need," he told her as he crossed his arms over his chest.

"I thought William was chief?"

"William died six months ago. I am now chief."

Her confusion was readily apparent.

"Ye dunnae ken?" he asked.

"Nay." That much was true. Since none ever came to call on them —save for the lying, cheating Darwud—living so far away and with Grueber's reputation as it was, they were not privy to much information.

"Why are ye here lookin' fer work?" he asked.

She took note that the angry tone had faded. "Me da died this past spring, so I thought to seek work here. Since ye have none, I shall be on me way. "

"Where do ye plan to go?" he asked.

In truth, she did not rightly know. "Mayhap another clan will take me in. Mayhap the Mackintoshes, if they still be our allies."

"They are," he told her, "but why do ye nae wish to stay here, amongst yer own people?"

*Well now the answer to that would take an entire day to give ye.* Not wishing to discuss the matter, she said, "I'll be leavin' now if ye don't mind." Once again, she tried to hand him the sleeping babe. Again, he refused to take her.

Another long moment of deafening silence passed between them.

"There may be no work in the kitchens, but I am in desperate need of someone to care fer me daughter," he said with a nod toward the sleeping babe.

"Pardon?" she said, uncertain she had heard him correctly.

"I need someone to care for me daughter. Would you be interested?"

He wasn't running for guards, wasn't searching for suspected stolen items, wasn't cursing her for being here, or for simply being Grueber's daughter. Instead, he was offering her the opportunity to care for her own babe. For the longest moment, she didn't know what to think or say.

"Well?" he asked. "Would ye be willin' to do it?"

"Ye dunnae ken me," she said. "Why would ye entrust yer daughter to a complete stranger?"

'Twas then his lips turned into a warm smile. Though she'd sworn off men the moment she found herself with child last year, this one— this one was enough to tempt her to reconsider.

"I have many reasons, lass. One bein' me daughter is sleepin' contentedly in yer arms, somethin' she has nae done since arrivin' here," he told her. "That alone is invaluable to me. I think she be a good judge of character, even at this tender age."

Was that a compliment? Having received so very few in her life, so few that she could not recall a single one, she was uncertain.

"And I do ken who ye are lass," he said, his smile still warm and kind.

*And ye be nae kickin' me out o' the keep?*

"Now, I will ask ye again, would ye be willin' to care fer me daughter?"

Her heart filled with so much joy that she could barely contain her smile. "'Twould be me great privilege!" Tamping down her excitement, she glanced at Nola. "She be a right beautiful babe."

"I would have to agree," Connor said before rubbing his hands together. "Will this room do?"

"Do fer what?"

"For yer quarters, lass. I'll need ye as close to her as possible, ye ken? Would ye like me to send someone to yer croft to gather yer things?"

'Twas laughable, but he had no way of knowing that. "All me things be in that bundle on the floor by her basket. But ye might send someone fer the cow and chickens."

He left the room and returned a moment later, holding the bundle up with a most confused expression. "This be *all* yer things?"

"Aye, m'laird," she told him.

As pitiful as her worldly possessions were, she could not remove the smile from her face.

"Verra well, then."

"Thank ye, m'laird, thank ye so verra much," she told him excitedly.

"Thank *ye*, lass, fer helpin' me. I fear I dunnae have much experience with bairns, therefore I shall forever be in your debt."

Her face grew warm. No one had ever been in her debt before.

"Where would ye like the chair?" he asked as he picked it up with one hand.

"Near the window would be welcome."

He set the chair at an angle. Little bits of dust danced in the sunlight shining in. She thanked him again.

"I'll have someone set up a brazier for ye. I'll also have me brothers bring in a bed, and a chest to hold yer things, and anythin' else ye might need."

Words weren't sufficient to show the amount of gratitude bursting in her heart.

"Now, shall we discuss recompense?"

Onnleigh was perplexed, felt her cheeks flame bright with embarrassment. "I fear I dunnae ken what that be."

"Payment for yer work," he explained.

Her eyes grew wide. "Ye wish to pay me?"

"Of course!" he exclaimed. "I would nae expect ye to work for free."

She laughed then, for the first time in an age. "M'laird, as long as I have a roof over me head and one hot meal a day, I will be verra happy."

*Besides, ye're given me daughter a home, a lovin' home, and fer that, I would work me fingers to the bone from sun-up to sundown to repay ye.*

He cleared his throat. "Lass, we eat three times a day here."

"One will be fair enough m'laird, fer I would nae want to be beholden to ye fer more."

A rather strange expression fell over his face, as if he were struggling with something. "I think I shall see to furnishings now. Will ye be all right here for a time?"

She nodded enthusiastically. "Aye, I will."

He gave a nod and slight bow before quitting the room.

THERE WAS NOT a doubt in his mind who Onnleigh truly was. He might not have known everything about her, but he was certain she was the babe's mother. The moment he stepped into the doorway and watched from the shadows, he was quickly able to put the pieces of the puzzle together.

To begin with, on the first afternoon when he discovered the babe, Braigh had come to his study. That was when his brother saw the child for the first time. When he saw the little tufts of red hair, he declared, "I think I ken who she might belong to."

He went on to explain to Connor and Ronald what he had witnessed at the wishing well. "She was a right pretty girl, with auburn hair. That basket," he said with a nod toward where it sat on Connor's desk, "was at her feet."

"Do ye ken who she be?" Connor had asked.

"Nay, but there was somethin' familiar about her. I do ken she is not someone we see here often. I dunnae ken her name, just that she be familiar."

Deciding it best to keep things quiet for a time, he sent his brothers out again to see what they could learn about the fiery red-haired lass. As of that very morning, they were no closer to learning who she truly was.

Secondly, he watched from the shadows as she fed the babe at her own breast.

When she'd introduced herself, it took a moment for recollection to set in. Grueber... the name was familiar. Why did he know that name? He hadn't heard it recently, of that he was certain. Tossing the name around his mind once more, recognition set in. Grueber MacCallen. A drunkard and thief who would steal the nails out of a wall if he thought he could make any money from it.

A quick glance at the clothes she wore—an old brown tunic over a coarse green skirt with many patches, hanging loosely on a small frame that had not seen good food in some time—told much. She had not been well cared for in her life, the knowledge made him angry.

And then, when she declared that all her worldly possessions were in that small bundle? Aye, as poor as dirt she was. But no amount of poverty could take away from her beauty. He had not been attracted to another woman since his sweet Maire. But this wee lass, with her auburn locks and bright blue eyes and smile that lit the room like the midday sun? She stirred something deep within him, something that had been dormant and quiet for far too long.

Why could he not remember seeing her within the walls or in the village outside the keep? Not wanting to embarrass her, he decided to not ask that burning question. Nay, he'd find out what he needed to know through other methods.

So he left her in the small room off his bedchamber and immediately went in pursuit of his brothers. He'd assign Ronald to keep a close eye on her. Not because he didn't trust her, but because he worried she would take the babe and leave. From the dark circles under her eyes and how scrawny she appeared, he did not think she'd last long on her own.

# CHAPTER 4

*R*onald was easy enough to find. He was in the gathering room eating while pretending *not* to be interested in Bridgett. With a roll of his eyes, Connor pulled his youngest brother away from the table, gave him a quick summation of what was happening and asked him to watch the girl closely.

"Ye really think she be the babe's mum?" Ronald asked as he took a healthy bite from the roasted chicken leg he held in his hand. How anyone could eat as much as Ronald did and remain as thin as he did, was a mystery to Connor.

"Aye, I do. But I want ye to keep that to yerself. Ye tell no one."

He nodded as he chewed. "I'll tell no one, ye have me word."

Connor thanked him. "Have ye seen Braigh?"

Ronald grinned mischievously. "He be above stairs with his wife. Ye might want to give him about a half an hour."

Connor shook his head and rested his hands on his hips. "I swear he will kill himself if he does nae stay away from her for at least a day."

Ronald laughed heartily. "I think he'd argue he'd die if he did."

Connor left Ronald to go in search of men to bring a bed, trunk, and other things from the storage room in the north tower. Standing in the shadows near the kitchens, he found Bridgett, who was pretending not to be interested in Ronald.

"Bridgett, I have a favor to ask ye."

She was easily startled, this one. She jumped, squealed in fright, before grabbing her chest with her hands. "Connor! Ye nearly scared me out of me skin!"

*If ye hadn't been so focused on me brother...* "I be sorry, lass."

Taking her by the elbow gently, he drew her out of the shadows. The petite, pretty girl with light brown hair and hazel eyes had been in love with his brother for years. She simply hadn't gotten up the courage to tell him yet, or anyone else. But everyone in the keep knew how she felt, for there was no mistaking it. At each meal, she saved the best cuts of meat, the warmest slice of bread, the freshest fruits for Ronald. She had a distinct look of awe and longing whenever she glanced his way. Hopefully, they'd both get up the courage to admit how they felt before they died of auld age.

"What is it ye need?" she asked as she tried to catch her breath.

"I have found someone to care for me daughter," he informed her. "She be above stairs with her now. Could ye help settle her in? See that she has everythin' she needs?"

"Och! I be so glad ye found someone," she smiled up at him. "Of course I shall help. Who is she?"

"Her name be Onnleigh."

Bridgett repeated the name a few times, searching for some memory. After a few moments, her eyes grew wide. "Nae Grueber's daughter?"

Connor nodded. "I ken he was a drunkard but I dunnae believe Onnleigh to be anything like him."

Lowering her voice, she motioned for Connor to draw nearer. "Grueber is more than a drunkard, he be a thief as well," she explained. "Do ye remember the time yer da caught him tryin' to steel a sheep?"

Connor searched his mind for some memory but could not find it.

"I was just a little girl then, but I remember it. Yer da caught him red-handed. Grueber lied his way out of it by sayin' the sheep had escaped and he was only tryin' to return it. He was famous for *findin'* things people had *lost*. Why yer da put up with him, I dunnae ken." She shook her head in disgust. "I've nae seen Onnleigh in at least ten years, mayhap more. We used to hold our pouches close when we saw Grueber comin'. I have nae seen him in at least a year."

Aye, Grueber's reputation was well known. While instinct warned him he should not trust Onnleigh completely. Still, he wondered if the apple didn't fall far from the tree. Was the daughter as big a thief as her father? But why should that be true? He dismissed the thought from his mind.

"Ye'll need nae worry about Grueber. He passed away last winter."

"I wish I could say I was sorry to hear it," she admitted.

"What of Onnleigh? What do ye ken of her?"

"I fear I dunnae ken her well at all. As I said, I have nae seen her in at least ten years. I do remember her bein' so quiet as a child. Her mum died when we were verra young. After that, she did nae visit verra often."

Ten years was an awfully long time to stay away from the keep and the village. Connor wondered if by chance she had stayed away out of shame. And who had fathered her babe? The more questions he asked, the more questions he found.

"Thank ye, Bridgett."

"Ye be welcome. Would ye like me to go to her now?"

He gave a nod of affirmation. "I would, thank ye."

They parted ways: Bridgett off to help Onnleigh and he to see if Braigh was done with his wife yet.

WHILE THE MEN brought in the furniture, Onnleigh did her best to stay out of their way. Finding a spot in the corner of Connor's room, she held Nola close. She had three days of being away from her daughter to make up for. As the men were busy setting up the bed, Bridgett entered the room. With a bright smile, she went to Onnleigh and introduced herself.

"I be Bridgett *ingen* Comnal," she said. "Connor tells me ye will be takin' care of his babe."

Unaccustomed to people being polite to her, Onnleigh simply smiled and gave a short nod. She had no recollection of having met the young woman before, certain that *had* they met in the past, Bridgett wouldn't be behaving so politely.

"I was takin' care of the wee babe until this morn," Bridgett told her. "But I had to get back to me sewin'. She is a bonny babe, aye?"

"Aye," Onnleigh answered, her voice nothing more than an unsteady whisper.

"Ye be Onnleigh *ingen* Grueber, aye?" Bridgett asked, taking her attention away from the babe for only a brief moment.

"Aye."

"I have nae seen ye in years. Why have ye stayed away so long?"

Her tone was not accusatory or harsh. 'Twas nothing more than a question born out of curiosity. Apparently Bridgett had little memory of how Onnleigh had been treated the last time she was at the keep. "I was busy takin' care o' me da."

Bridgett studied her closely for a time. "I be glad ye're here, Onnleigh. I hope we can become good friends."

Tears welled and there was nothing to be done for it. In the whole of her life, Onnleigh could not ever remember having a friend. "I would like that verra much."

"'Twill be time for the noonin' meal soon," Bridgett said. "Would ye like to sit with me?"

Not quite ready yet to be reintroduced to the clan that had ostracized her years ago, she politely declined. "I think I would like to put me room in order." 'Twas the only excuse she could think of.

"Then I shall bring a meal to you," Bridgett said with a smile. "I will help ye put yer room in order as well."

Doubt plagued Onnleigh. Had Connor sent Bridgett to watch over her? To make certain she didn't steal anything? There would be no way of getting her to leave if that was the case. "That would be verra nice," she said.

Soon the men declared the bed assembled and left the two women alone.

"Connor has ye stayin' next to him?" Bridgett asked as she headed toward the small room.

Onnleigh followed her. "Aye. He says he needs me close to N—" she stopped short of speaking the babe's name. No doubt, Connor had already given her a new one. "The babe."

Bridgett stood in the middle of the tiny room and gave it a quick inspection. "We'll need rugs, fresh linens, more linens and nappies for the babe."

Rugs? Fresh linens? 'Twould be a most welcome change compared to how she'd been living, however she felt wholly unworthy of anyone going out of their way. "No need to fuss over me," she said. "A warm blanket or two and I'll be verra happy. Give the babe the things she needs."

Pretending not to hear her protests, Bridgett went on to say, "Mayhap a tapestry or two on the walls? The room be far too dark. A babe needs lots of bright colors and sunshine, aye?"

Truly, as long as they were providing the things Nola needed, Onnleigh cared for naught else. But how could she explain what she truly felt without giving away that she was the babe's mum?

Bridgett left to get them lunch, with the promise that she would return soon. Onnleigh breathed a sigh of relief at finally being alone. She stood in the middle of the room and looked at her surroundings. 'Twas a very nice room, so much nicer than where she had been raised. 'Twas then she realized her heart felt *light*. So much lighter and at ease than she could ever remember feeling.

*Ye best nae get yerself too comfortable,* a little voice warned. *As soon as they remember who ye be, they will nae be so nice.*

BRIDGETT HAD RETURNED QUICKLY, and with more food than Onnleigh could remember enjoying in an age. "All this food, just fer us?" she asked, in awe at the roast venison, vegetables, bread, cheese, apples and berries, and tankards of cider.

From the expression on Bridgett's face, she thought Onnleigh's question odd, but kindly enough, she did not remark.

They sat opposite one another at the little table, while the babe slept in the cradle not far from Onnleigh's feet. She could not remember a time in her life when she experienced such delicious food, nor could she ever remember being in the presence of someone who talked as much as Bridgett.

"I ken it has been some time since ye've been in the keep," she began. "Much has changed over the years."

Onnleigh gave a slight nod of understanding. "Aye, Connor be the chief now. I dinnae ken William had passed."

"William, Connor's mum, his wife and babe as well, all within the past four years."

Onnleigh felt a tug of regret at hearing the news about his wife and babe. "I dinnae ken he had married."

"Aye, they were married less than a year. 'Twas such a difficult time fer him. He loved Maire verra much."

Her eyes widened in surprise. "Maire?"

Bridgett laughed. "Aye, *Maire*, Helen's eldest daughter. Though I must tell ye, Maire was much nicer than her mum or her sister, Margaret. Och! Never have I met two women as cold-hearted as they."

Helen. She had been the woman who had taken the switch to Onnleigh's rear end and legs that day more than ten years ago. It had been *Helen's* garden she had taken the leeks from. An involuntary shudder traced up and down her spine at the memory.

"Connor's brother, Braigh be married now, to a verra fine woman. She's with child, and due in a few months. Ronald, his other brother, he is nae married."

Onnleigh was still trying to get rid of the vision of Helen whipping her out of the gates, not really paying attention to much of what Bridgett was saying. And poor Connor. Having lost his wife and babe.

"Louisa, she be in charge of the kitchens now, and a verra nice woman. If ye ever need anythin' and ye cannae find me, just ask Louisa."

"How did Connor's wife and babe die?" she asked.

Bridgett's smile faded. "'Twas so verra sad. The babe came much too early. Maire died just a few hours after birthin' him. He died the followin' morn."

Dying alone, in childbirth, had been one of the things she had worried about when she was carrying Nola. Her biggest fear was that she would give birth to a living babe only to die minutes later, leaving her babe all alone in this world, with no one to care for her.

Before they had finished their meal, Nola began to stir. Onnleigh went to her immediately, lifted her out of the cradle and to her chest. "How be our bright babe?" she asked soothingly.

Nola looked up at her before thrusting her fist into her mouth. Onnleigh's heart felt near to bursting, she was so thankful and happy to be reunited with her child. But that little voice still warned against becoming too at ease among these people.

LATER IN THE afternoon Onnleigh was summoned to Connor's study, with the request that she bring the babe with her.

When she had first entered the keep that morning, no one had paid much attention to her. However, when Bridgett led the way to the study, she could not help but feel a distinct difference in attitude toward her. Though none uttered a word, those few people in the gathering room glared at her with piercing gazes and pursed lips as if to say, *We do nae want ye here.*

She had been correct in her presumption that once word began to spread, the mistrust her clanspeople felt toward her would come begin to show. It made her skin cold, turning it to gooseflesh with each step she took.

Bridgett left her just outside Connor's door with a promise to see her at the evening meal. If what she had just witnessed were any indication of how these people felt about her, she would prefer to keep to her room.

She rapped lightly on the door as she prayed silently for her legs to stop shaking.

"Come!" Connor's voice boomed from within.

With Nola in one arm, Onnleigh slowly opened the door and stepped inside.

He was sitting behind a grand desk with candles all ablaze, even though a good amount of sunlight streamed in through the open windows. Candles had been a rare commodity as she grew up, and she could not see much sense in burning them in broad daylight. Still, 'twasn't her coin they were burning, so she kept her thoughts on the matter to herself.

"Ah! Onnleigh," Connor said when he looked up from the large, open book before him. "How be ye this fine afternoon?"

Instantly, she relaxed. He seemed genuinely happy to see her, unlike the folks in the gathering room. "I be well, thank ye."

"And yer room? Are ye settled in to yer likin'?" His lips curved into a warm smile that formed creases around his eyes. Eyes that near sparkled with kindness.

"Aye, I have, m'laird." Try as she might, she could not resist the urge to return his smile.

He gave an approving nod before motioning her forward. "Come, I wish to show ye somethin'."

Cautiously—out of habit more than any true fear of the man—she stepped forward.

He waved her to come around the desk and stand beside him.

"Do ye ken what this is?" he asked as he tapped a finger on one of the open pages.

"A book?" she answered, feeling rather silly, for anyone could see 'twas a book. A very large and thick book.

"Aye, a book. But this be a verra special book."

She waited silently for further explanation.

"This book be more than one hundred years old, and some of the pages within be even older," he said. "Since the day Clan MacCallen was formed, the chiefs have been enterin' the names of their people. When they were born, who they were born to, who they married, any children they may have had, as well as the day they died."

'Twas the entire history of their clan laid out before him. He seemed quite proud of it, so she offered him a warm smile, not quite understanding why he was showing it to her.

With his index finger, he pointed to one entry in particular. "See?"

Aye, she could see it, but it didn't mean she understood what the markings were. All at once, she felt embarrassed as a crimson blush rose from her neck to the top of her head. "I cannae read it," she whispered.

He looked up with a furrowed brow. "Ye cannae read?"

She thought he sounded as surprised as he did disgusted, causing her embarrassment to deepen.

"Did yer parents nae teach ye?"

She gave a slight shake of her head. "Me mum showed me what me name looked like once, but that was a long time ago."

'Twas his turn to look embarrassed. "I be sorry, Onnleigh. I forgot yer mum died."

"I was five," she told him, as if that explained fully her lack of education.

He turned his attention back to the markings on the page. "This be ye," he said as he ran his finger under the markings. "Onnleigh, born to Claire and Grueber, May 14, year of our Lord, fourteen hundred aught six."

Her brow furrowed as she leaned in for a better look, as if that would somehow bring some clarity to the beautiful lines on the page. "That be when I was born?" she asked.

He turned to look at her, his face just inches from her own. Onnleigh noticed then just how deep a green his eyes were. Dark, like summer grass. A tickling sensation formed in her stomach, one she'd felt only once before. That sensation had led her to where she now stood. It took a great deal of effort to look away, but she knew that she must. Standing upright, she made a silent promise not to stare at him again.

49

"Did ye nae celebrate the anniversary of yer birth?" he asked her. His voice sounded scratchy, as if he was quite thirsty.

Casting him a curious look, she said, "Nae, do ye?"

"Aye, we do. We celebrate many things here," he told her. She could feel his eyes were still upon her.

"Such as?"

"Weddings and births throughout the year. And at the moment, we be readying for Yuletide." His voice trailed away.

"I remember a Yule right before me mum passed," she said while she tried to recall as much as she could about that time. "There was a big log ablaze in the fire. And I think I remember gettin' a sweet cake." 'Twas one of the very few happy memories she had from her childhood, even if it was fragmented and faded.

A long stretch of silence fell between them before Connor spoke again. "I want to add the babe's name to the book." He flipped through the pages until he found the one he was looking for. "But I dunnae ken what to call her."

Onnleigh felt her chest tighten with fear. Did he know the truth?

A moment later, he turned to the babe in her arms and smiled fondly. "She be a beautiful lass, aye?"

Onnleigh nodded in agreement.

"I like the name Maureen, but I fear she does nae look like a *Maureen*. Elsbeth mayhap? Or Eliza?" he shook his head. "Nae, none of those seem to suit her. What do ye think?"

She swallowed the knot of trepidation back. Was he asking her opinion or laying a trap? At the moment, she couldn't judge. Feigning ignorance, she looked down at her sleeping babe and smiled. "I think she looks like a *Nola*, to me."

"Nola," he spoke the name twice more. "I think ye be right, lass. Nola be a fine name and Nola, it shall be."

He turned back to the book, dabbed a quill into the jar of ink and began to write. "N, o, l, a," he said, spelling the name aloud as he wrote. "I fear we dunnae ken the true date she was born. She looks to be only a few weeks old."

*Three months and five days to be exact.*

"I dunnae ken who her mum or da be. I shall put me own name as her da's."

Onnleigh's heart soared with gratitude while a question burned, begging to be asked. "Be that fer ferever?"

Connor turned and smiled. "Aye, lass, that be forever. From this day forward, I shall be her da. 'Twill never change."

Tears welled, but she held them back as she turned away. 'Twas all Onnleigh wanted for her babe: a man who would gladly claim Nola as his own, even if he didn't want *her mother*. Her child would have a much brighter future, better than anything she could have given her, no matter how much she loved her. With her back to him, she asked, "Why do ye do that? Take a babe, nae kennin' who she be or who her parents be?"

Before Connor could answer, she heard a woman's voice come from behind her.

"So it be true."

ONNLEIGH SPUN to see Helen standing just inside the doorway. And she did not look the least bit happy.

Ignoring Onnleigh, she went to Connor. "Nae only do ye refuse to listen to me about keepin' *that* child, now ye've gone and hired the thief's daughter to care for it!"

"Need I remind ye that I be chief of this clan? I do nae need yer permission to do anything," Connor told her, his words clipped, his tone firm.

Helen scoffed. "Ye might nae need my permission, but ye should heed me good advice."

"If I heeded *yer* advice, I'd have married Margaret the day after I buried me wife and son!" He had reached the ends of his patience. For four years, he'd bitten his tongue, tried being thoughtful and kind with this woman, but he'd had enough.

"Bah! I'd have given ye a full year to mourn. And what be wrong with Margaret? She'd make ye a good wife. Ye ken it. I do nae understand why ye keep fightin' it. And I cannae understand why ye'd take in a bastard child, and bring the daughter of a thief into me home."

Connor jumped to his feet, his face purple with rage. "This is *Clan MacCallen's* home, its keep, and its lands. Onnleigh is a MacCallen and she has just as much right to be here as any of us. Whatever her father may have done is nae a reflection upon her. It will serve ye well to remember that. I am keeping Nola as me daughter and Onnleigh as her nurse."

"Ye've named it?" Helen exclaimed.

"Aye, I've named *her* and I've claimed her."

He said it with such pride, with such conviction that even Onnleigh began to believe he could love the child just as much as if she were his own.

Helen glared at him, her hands on her hips, her disgust quite apparent. "Ye'll regret this, Connor. Mark me words."

"Ye need to apologize to Onnleigh fer bein' so rude."

From the expression on Helen's face, one would have thought he'd just slapped her. "I have nothin' to apologize fer. Contrary to what ye might think, I do have only yer best interests in me heart."

Connor had known this woman all his life. He knew the only interests she ever had in her heart were her own. "If ye wish to remain in me good graces, ye will apologize to Onnleigh now. She has done nothing to deserve yer unkind mistreatment." On this, he would give no quarter.

"Verra well, then," she said before turning to face Onnleigh. "I apologize if I said anythin' to upset ye."

There was no sincerity in her tone, but at least she had uttered the words. With a graceful inclination of her head toward Connor, she quit the room. Her anger hung in the air long after she left.

'Twas the first time Onnleigh could ever recall someone standing up for her. Was it out of pity, or some deeply felt sense of honor and kindness? Either way, she was grateful for his insistence that Helen apologize.

"I be sorry for the way Helen behaved," Connor told her. "I fear she has the misguided notion that her opinion and only hers is important."

All Onnleigh could think to do was thank him. "I thank ye kindly," she said.

It was becoming increasingly difficult to look into those warm, green eyes of his, without her stomach feeling as if it were full of birds wanting to take flight. "Nola needs changin'," she told him after several long moments passed between them.

Without waiting for permission, she quit the room in a rush.

# CHAPTER 5

*H*aving been isolated from the world for as long as she had, Onnleigh was fearful of leaving her tiny room. While Connor might be kind enough to overlook who sired her, she was confident the rest of the clan would not. She spent the remainder of the day and night above stairs, tending to Nola and being thankful for a roof over her head, food in her belly, and all the lovely things Connor had made certain they were given.

While she sat next to her brazier, the sound of all the joyful people supping together below stairs floated into her room. Feelings she believed had been buried long ago began to rise deep inside her. Longing, envy, and loneliness. Memories of her childhood, of always being left alone to watch as the other children played together, began to surge into her mind. She had desperately wanted to play with the others, but didn't know how to ask. Whether out of shyness or fear, she couldn't say.

That was not the kind of childhood she wanted for her daughter. Nay, Nola deserved to be surrounded by people who loved her. She deserved to grow up happy, with many friends, to have hundreds of happy childhood memories to carry her into her auld age. Onnleigh wanted everything for her babe that she had never had.

Sitting next to the brazier, she looked into the cradle at her sleeping dear one, her heart heavy and filled with regrets. No matter how strong her desire to shout to the world that she, Onnleigh ingen Grueber of Clan MacCallen, had created such a sweet, beautiful babe, she knew she could not. 'Twould mean the end of any chance of the decent life her daughter had miraculously been blessed with.

The sound of Connor's deep voice broke through her silent reverie. "Onnleigh?" he all but whispered her name as he stepped out of the shadows. "Why did ye nae come below stairs to sup?"

She looked up at him with a curious expression. He truly did not understand her reluctance. "'Tis awfully loud down there." 'Twasn't necessarily a complete lie, for she was used to silence. Being around loud, boisterous, happy people was foreign to her.

A warm smile lit his face as he stared down at Nola. "She is a beautiful babe, is she nae?"

A knot of regret formed in her throat. She wondered if her father had once looked upon her with the same kind of adoration. 'Twas doubtful.

"Ye needn't stay up here all the time," Connor said, turning his attention away from Nola.

*Och, ye daft, sweet man, but I must!*

"Many of the women folk come to sew in the gatherin' room this time of year. Mayhap ye should join them." His tone was quite sincere, his eyes alight with hope.

Though his suggestion was born of kindness, she believed it awfully naive. "I do nae think ye understand the way of it, m'laird," she told him. "Yer people do nae like me."

"They're yer people too," he said, his voice low and warm.

She did not want to insult his intelligence—or lack thereof—on the matter, but there was no other way around it. "They're nae me people. They've ne'er been me people."

Thankfully, he did not argue, did not call her daft or silly for having such feelings. "They'll never be yer people unless ye give them a chance to know ye. Nae all of them are like Helen and Margaret."

She could only agree with him, inasmuch as he and Bridgett had been quite kind. Mayhap, just mayhap there were more MacCallen's like them and far fewer like Helen.

"Give them a chance, Onnleigh. Give yerself a chance to show them ye be the kind and sweet lass I ken ye to be."

RELUCTANTLY, Onnleigh decided to at least make an attempt at reintroducing herself to her clanspeople as Connor had suggested the night before. The morning had dawned gloomily, with dark gray skies and rain that pounded against the walls of the keep. An omen, mayhap, of things to come.

She scrubbed her face, washed her teeth, and ran her wooden comb through her hair. Her best dress was the blue wool, for it had the least number of patches and stains. Since she had used the only chemise to her name to make gowns for Nola, she was forced to use her tunic as a replacement. The brown didn't necessarily go with the blue, but at least it covered her arms.

With Nola wrapped in the sling and her shawl draped around her shoulders, she took several deep breaths before descending the stairs into the already crowded gathering room. She scanned the large space, looking for Connor, who had left his bedchamber before dawn. He was nowhere to be seen. Neither was Bridgett.

Pushing aside a sense of dread, she held her head high, her babe close, and went to the long table against the wall. Eggs, ham, breads, cheeses, jams, fruits and food she couldn't remember seeing before were spread out, free for the taking. Her mouth watered as her stomach growled. A sudden hush fell over the room as she picked up a trencher.

*'Tis nae stealin' if 'tis fer all,* she told herself. Her fingers trembled as she placed a slice of ham on the trencher. She could feel all eyes in the room boring through her skull. Not wanting to appear gluttonous or greedy, she took small portions of eggs, one slice of bread, a tiny hunk of cheese and a few sliced apples. Knots formed in the pit of her

stomach when she turned away from the table and saw a room full of people staring at her.

*Mayhap 'tis nae fer all,* that small, doubtful voice warned. She was about to set the trencher down on the nearest table and flee to her room when Bridgett appeared beside her. "Good morn, to ye," she said happily as she took her by the elbow. "Come, let us go above stairs to eat. The room has a chill and we would nae want the babe to catch a cough."

Naive as she may be, she knew exactly what Bridgett was doing: saving her from the glowers and harsh whispers of people who did not want her here.

Trembling, she allowed Bridgett to guide her up to her room.

"The rain has cast a chill everywhere," Bridgett said as they sat at the small table. "I be certain 'twill nae last long, ye ken."

Onnleigh felt numb, her appetite gone, the knots in her stomach tightening. "Why do they hate me so?" she asked, her voice so low 'twas barely discernible to Bridgett.

"Och, they dunnae hate ye," Bridgett replied, as if nothing were further from the truth.

"They do," Onnleigh said as she stared at the cold brazier. Tears built, but she refused to shed them.

Bridgett sighed in defeat. "Onnleigh, I dunnae believe they hate ye, they just dunnae ken ye. Give it time, show them that ye be nothin' like yer da. And do nae hold yer head in shame. Stand proud and show them who ye are. We have a good clan, filled with good people. Ye'll see, with time, they'll get to ken ye and ye them and all will be good."

Mayhap those below stairs hadn't been looking at her with hatred, but with curiosity. It had been an age since any had seen her. In truth, she was more a stranger than anything. Was it at all possible she had misread all those faces? 'Twas true that she was not accustomed to being around anyone save her father, and then that cheat and liar Darwud.

Mayhap not everyone behaved as they had.

Mayhap if she did what Bridgett and Connor were suggesting, she might just find a place here.

~

ONNLEIGH HAD GIVEN much thought to what Bridgett and Connor had been telling her; the clan could not change their minds about her if she stayed to her room. The only way to get them to see she was nothing at all like her father, was to show them.

The next morn dawned just as gloomy as the day before, with leaden skies and much rain. Refusing to allow the weather to darken her spirits, she tended to Nola first, before slipping back into her blue gown and brown tunic. She had washed both out the night before and thankfully, they were both dry. She made herself as presentable as possible before slipping Nola into her sling and going downstairs.

This morn, she held her head high, but not so high anyone might think her haughty. She offered a warm smile to anyone who had the courage to look her in the eye. The sideboard was laden with the same kind of foods it had been yesterday. Onnleigh prepared a trencher and turned to find a table at which she could sit.

She was met with the same icy glowers and harsh whispers as the day before. Knots grew in her stomach and her fingers began to tremble. *Calm yerself,* she told her rapidly beating heart. *Show them ye be nae like yer da.*

Taking a deep breath, she went to the nearest table where men and women of various ages sat. A few took one look at her and began to spread out, taking up any free space. Their actions said more than words ever could: *ye cannae sit here.*

She was met with the same cold shoulders, grunts, and snorts of derision at the next two tables. And everyone spread out to make certain she could not sit. The knots grew larger, destroying any appetite she previously had.

She scanned the room for any sign of a welcoming face. There was not one. Some pretended she wasn't standing just steps away. Others continued with their hate-filled glowers.

Bridgett was not here to rescue her this morn, to take her by the arm and whisk her above stairs to the safety of her little room. It had been a very long while since she felt this alone amongst so many. As much as she wanted to cry, she refused. *Show them,* she heard Connor's voice in the back of her mind. *Show them.*

Taking in a deep, steadying breath, she scanned the room once more. There was one small empty table in the corner of the room. Lifting her chin ever so slightly, refusing to allow them to see her pain, she sat alone there, with her back to the rest of the people.

Quietly, she ate her meal, wishing for all the world that Connor or Bridgett would suddenly appear. She felt a sense of safety whenever she was with them. More so with Connor.

Occasionally, she heard her name whispered. She could only make out every other word. Just enough to cause her heart to crack a little more. *The thief's daughter ... guard yer purse ... what be Connor thinkin', havin' her here?*

With her appetite gone, she ate only because she knew she had to. She forced down a few bites of bread and one egg, and could take no more. Leaving her half eaten trencher behind, she slowly made her way to her room. Would they ever trust and accept her? Had she hidden herself away far too long?

'Twasn't until she was inside her small room that she let the tears fall.

After a time, she realized she was feeling sorry for herself. "What does it matter?" she asked the shadows. "Ye have been alone the whole of yer life. Ye should be used to this by now."

Sitting on the small chair, she slowly rocked Nola to sleep. Looking at her sweet babe, some of the heartache began to wane. "Our plight could be much worse," she murmured. "Da could still be alive and we could still be livin' with him."

That thought alone was the only thing that made her feel better about her situation.

AND SO IT repeated for the next three mornings. Onnleigh would go below stairs, fix a trencher for herself, and attempt to sit with someone. *Anyone.* However, these people were still behaving as if she were a murderer. Not one would allow her to join them.

The nooning meals were spent in her room with Bridgett. Her evening meals were spent with Connor, hidden away in her little room, pretending naught a thing was wrong in her world. Onnleigh looked forward to this part of the day most of all, for she had Connor all to herself. They were getting to know one another better with each passing day.

She refused to tell Connor or Bridgett what was happening. Eventually, they would both come to the same conclusion as she: no one wanted her here.

*Let them be rude,* she told herself on this, the fourth morning. With her head held high, she prepared a trencher. But this morn, she refused to stand at each table in hopes someone would allow her to sit. Instead, she took her place at the small table.

"Be ye Onnleigh?" came a man's voice from behind.

She spun around, her heart filled with more than just a bit of fear and dread. She found no malice in the man's eyes, or in those belonging to the pretty woman standing next to him. He was nearly as tall as Connor, with the same blonde hair and bright green eyes. The woman was beautiful, her auburn hair plated around her head. There was a warmth to her dark green eyes that made Onnleigh's fear and trepidation fall away at once.

"I did nae mean to startle ye," he said with a smile. "I be Braigh, Connor's younger brother. This be me wife, Lorna."

Relief washed over her as she let her breath out in a quiet whoosh, so glad was she to see someone with a warm smile.

"Could we sit with ye?" Braigh asked with a hopeful expression.

"That would be right nice," Onnleigh murmured.

"'Tis nice to finally meet ye," he said as he helped his wife onto the bench across from Onnleigh.

"I have heard many nice things about ye," Lorna added with a smile.

Before Onnleigh could reply, Braigh asked his wife if there was anything in particular she wanted to eat this morn. "Eggs," she replied. "Lots and lots of eggs."

Braigh chuckled, gave her a nod, and stepped away.

Lorna placed a palm on her stomach and smiled at Onnleigh. "I dunnae ken why, but I have been cravin' eggs for weeks now." She giggled.

Onnleigh thought back to when she was carrying Nola. She craved many things back then. None of which she had any access to. But alas, those memories of that time were naught to be shared with anyone.

Lorna smiled warmly at Nola. "Connor be awfully proud of the wee one."

Onnleigh smiled proudly and agreed.

"My babe should arrive this spring," Lorna told her. "The midwife says mid-March."

"It be yer first?"

"Aye," she said, still smiling down at Nola. "Braigh is convinced it be a boy child, and I am tempted to agree. Only because he keeps me up all hours of the night, like his da."

Lorna's giggling increased when she saw the blush creep up Onnleigh's neck. "I be sorry," she said. "Ye will learn I rarely think before I speak."

Onnleigh was beginning to like this woman immensely.

Braigh returned with two trenchers, one filled with six hard-boiled eggs that he handed to his wife. "I will get ye more if ye need them," he said with a wink and a smile.

He settled in next to his wife and began to eat. Between bites, he said, "I fer one be right glad ye be able to take care of the babe. I ken Connor certainly is as well."

*Nae nearly as happy as I,* Onnleigh thought to herself.

"I do hope we can become good friends," Lorna told her with a hopeful smile.

"I would like that," Onnleigh replied. *Two friends in less than a sennight?* She quashed the urge to giggle like a fool.

For the next half hour, they talked, getting better acquainted with one another. She learned that Lorna was from the Mackintosh clan, both her parents having died several years ago.

"I do have a sister, Myrna. She still lives amongst the Mackintoshes, married she is. She is expectin' her third babe in February."

Onnleigh listened intently, glad she was to finally have someone else besides Bridgett or Connor to sup with. "How did ye and Braigh meet?" she asked curiously.

Braigh grinned and gave his wife a wink, before answering the question. "I first met and fell in love with me wife when I was a lad of no more than five and ten," he told her. "We met at a clan gathering at the Mackintosh keep. She was the most beautiful lass I'd ever seen. I decided then and there that someday, I'd make her me wife." The adoration in his eyes when he looked at his wife was enviable.

Lorna rolled her eyes and giggled. "Took him six long years to ask fer me hand," she explained to Onnleigh.

*At least he asked,* Onnleigh thought. *That be more than I could e'er hope fer.* Tamping down her envy, she smiled and listened.

"I wanted to make certain I could provide fer ye before I asked fer yer hand," he said with another mischievous wink.

Lorna leaned forward to speak directly to Onnleigh. "That is what he *says,*" she said playfully. "But methinks he was a bit too afraid of me da."

So it went, the playful banter betwixt a husband and wife. While she was quite grateful and happy for their company, Onnleigh made a silent wish that someday, before she was auld and gray, there would be someone special in her life. Someone with whom she could share playful moments like the ones betwixt this couple who were so obviously in love with one another. *Mayhap, someday.*

ONNLEIGH FELT MUCH BETTER after breaking her fast with Braigh and Lorna. Returning to her room, she lit the fire in her brazier before settling in to feed Nola. Her heart felt light, happy to have made friends with these new people.

With her spirits lifted, she set about tidying her room, although there was truly not much need for it. She kept everything in order, mostly out of habit, but also out of respect for Connor. He had done so much for her. Far more than anyone else had ever even attempted to do.

She pulled the fur away from her window to look outside. Just beyond the wall were tiny, well-kept cottages. Just beyond those, a large hill.

Picking Nola up from the cradle, Onnleigh brought her back to the window.

She pointed to things outside and explained what they were. "Those be tiny cottages where happy families live," she told her. "In all me life, 'twas all I ever hoped fer. A wee cottage with a roof that did nae leak. Now look at us, aye?"

She was startled when a knock sounded at her doorway. "Onnleigh?"

'Twas Braigh's voice coming from the shadows. "May I come in?"

Onnleigh gave him permission to enter, believing Lorna was with him.

Braigh offered her a sincere and warm smile. "I hate to bother ye, but I have a favor to ask."

Confused, she gave a slight nod of her head whilst she wondered where his wife was. She felt uncomfortable having any man save for Connor in her room.

"I have duties that will keep me away the rest of the day," he told her. "I was wonderin', could ye keep Lorna company this day? I worry about leavin' her alone."

She didn't understand why he was worried and wondered if Lorna had some affliction she should be made aware of.

Braigh laughed heartily when she asked. "Nay," he said with a shake of his head. "I simply worry about her gettin' lonely. Me and me brothers be the only family she has here."

The sincere concern in his eyes nearly brought tears to her own. Lord above, how wonderful it would be to have someone care so much!

"'Twould be me great honor," Onnleigh said with a smile. She felt proud and elated that Braigh would ask such a thing of her, for they'd only just met.

He blew out a relieved breath and thanked her. "We be down the hall and around the corner. First door on the right. I shall return before the evenin' meal."

# CHAPTER 6

*N*early a fortnight had passed since Onnleigh had arrived at
the keep. Much to Braigh's relief, Lorna and Onnleigh
had become fast friends. More than once he remarked how happy and
grateful he was to have Onnleigh there to keep his wife company so
that he could tend to his duties without worry. With each word of
thanks from him, Onnleigh began to stand a bit taller and to worry
far less.

As soon as they finished breaking their fasts, they would return to
Lorna's chamber where they would sew and talk for most of the day.
Often times, Bridget would join them. With her good instruction,
Onnleigh's stitches improved considerably.

She had yet to meet Ronald, Connor's youngest brother.
According to Bridgett, Ronald preferred the night watch and
patrolling their borders. If what Bridgett told her was true, then the
young man was perhaps the most handsome, kind, generous, and
perfect man to ever walk God's earth. Onnleigh wondered if Ronald
was as in love with Bridgett as Bridgett was with him?

Onnleigh and Nola fell into a comfortable schedule. Though
flagons of goats' milk was sent to her room several times each day,

there was no need for it. Not one to allow anything to go to waste, Onnleigh would drink it, leaving the empty flagon on the table.

Connor would come to see them before he left each morn. He was such a kind man and very attentive toward Nola. He would hold her and talk to her before heading off to do whatever work it was he had in store for the day.

At night, he would return with a meal he shared with Onnleigh. He would talk about his day, about the plans for the upcoming Yuletide, and the like. For the most part, Onnleigh would only listen, asking an occasional question, so as not to appear addlepated or inept. He would also talk about his childhood, about the time he fostered with the Mackintoshes, and of Maire.

Maire was the one true love of his life, there was no doubt of it. Onnleigh remembered her being a beautiful child, but naught else. She would have to have been a remarkable woman in order to catch Connor's attention and gain his heart. *Will anyone ever think of me the way Connor still thinks of Maire?* She often found herself wondering. Chances were nil; she knew that. As much as she tried willing her heart and mind away from such things, 'twas impossible. No one, and most assuredly no one as wonderful as Connor, would ever look upon her with loving and adoring eyes. And were she to die on the morrow, there would be no one to mourn her loss.

'Twas those thoughts that kept her awake at night. That, along with worry. If anyone were to find out she had given birth to Nola, Onnleigh's entire world would come to a screeching halt. Connor would undoubtedly send her away, for what man would want a woman of loose morals in his home? And what would happen to Nola? Would he keep her or would he insist Onnleigh take her away?

Those sleepless nights made her feel tired during the day. But the moment Connor walked into her room, all those worries fell away. He made her feel at peace. Safe and protected too.

There was no doubt in her mind that he cared a great deal for his clan and their future. He was a good, kind man. A man she was growing more fond of as the days passed.

This night, however, he seemed distracted. Worried it had something to do with her, she picked at her food until she could take no more. "What bothers ye this night?" she asked, feigning an air of calm.

Connor raked a hand through his blond hair as he set his eating knife down. "I have received word that the Randalls and the McCrearys are joinin' forces."

Though she had no true idea what it meant, she could see from the worry etched in his face 'twas not good news for the MacCallens. "I fear I dunnae understand," she admitted.

Connor let out a heavy breath of frustration. "We are well matched against either clan. But if they join forces, we will be sorely outnumbered."

A large knot formed in the pit of her stomach. "Will we be goin' to war?"

He pursed his lips together and shook his head. "I pray no'," he said woefully.

She did not know the first thing about war or battles. Only enough to be frightened at the possibility. "Are the Mackintoshes and McLarens still our allies?"

"Aye," he replied. "But they have problems of their own at the moment. They be warrin' with the MacRays."

"Why must men fight so? Why can we no' all just leave one another alone?"

He scoffed and shrugged his shoulders. "As long as evil exists in this world and as long as men thirst for power and hunger for *more,* then there will never be peace in this world."

There was no arguing against that.

They sat in quiet contemplation for a long while. With all her heart she wished she could help Connor as he had helped her and Nola. But what help could a poor, uneducated woman be to a man like him?

"What if ye joined forces with the Randalls before the McCrearys do?" she asked.

When he looked at her as if she were something he'd never seen before, she felt her face grow warm with shame. *It would serve ye well to learn to keep yer mouth shut,* she cursed inwardly.

"What do ye ken of the Randalls?" he asked with a raised brow.

With her shoulders slumped, she was afraid to answer. "Nae much, m'laird. I only ken they be our enemy."

"Aye, they are, and have been for so long no one can now remember why."

Setting her eating knife aside, she folded her hands in her lap. "I be sorry that I cannae help ye."

'Twas then he did the most unexpected of things. He took her hand in his and gave it a gentle squeeze. 'Twas the first time in many a year that anyone had done such a thing. She refused to count the intimate moments with Darwud, as they were born out of falsehoods.

Connor's skin felt warm against her own, setting her stomach to flip and flop excitedly. *Nay,* she warned her traitorous heart. *Do no' believe it be more than yer laird bein' kind.*

"But ye *have* helped me, Onnleigh. More than ye realize."

Dubious, she looked up with a raised brow. "Me? Helped ye?"

His smile was so warm and kind it made her feel … something she'd not ever felt before. Appreciated? Wanted?

"Aye, lass, ye have. Ye see, I feel at ease talkin' with ye. There are no' too many here I can talk to as I do ye. Ye be a verra good listener."

A good listener? While she knew he meant it as a compliment, her frantically beating heart wanted to scream that it wanted more.

"I consider ye my friend, Onnleigh."

'Twas said with such sincerity that she felt close to crying. *His friend? Aye, I can be his friend, for 'tis with a certainty I could never be more than that.* Mayhap as his friend, he would not turn his back on her when he learned all the secrets she had been keeping.

"So," he said as he picked up his eating knife again. "Ye think we should ally ourselves with the Randalls?"

Believing herself to be the last person he should come to for advice, she remained silent.

"Onnleigh?" he said her name with much concern.

"I fear I do no' ken the ways of warrin' and such, m'laird. Mayhap ye should ask someone who kens better than I."

"It has been me experience that those who *think* they ken the way of the world and what must be done, are no' always right. I would like to hear what *ye* think."

Taking in a slow, deep breath, she found the courage to answer. "I think the Randalls would be more trustworthy than the McCreary's as allies."

"Why?" he asked, with a raised brow.

"Well, me da was quite fond of the McCrearys. Kennin' me da as I did, it would lead me to believe they are about as trustworthy as he was."

He could find no fault in that argument. Letting loose with a low, soft chuckle, he scratched the back of his neck. The last thing he wanted to do was to insult her father. Even if he had been naught but a lying, thieving whoreson. "Ye may be right," he admitted to her.

"Well, I reckon the only way to find out would be to ask," she told him.

Connor could only pray it would be as simple as that.

As had become habit, Onnleigh broke her fast with Braigh and Lorna, then returned to her room to visit with Bridgett. She was grateful for Bridgett's friendship.

Over the many years alone, Onnleigh had often wished for a friend like Bridgett. Someone who'd not frown upon her tattered clothes, her poor speech, her lack of knowledge of worldly things.

"Well, I'd best be goin'," Bridgett finally announced. "I would love to spend the day with ye, but there is much work to be done."

If Nola hadn't started to fuss, signifying she'd soon be ready to eat, Onnleigh would have loved to argue for Bridgett stay. Onnleigh had grown used to her company and did not like being alone much anymore. "Do ye think I could help?" she asked as she lifted Nola from the cradle. "I be verra good at cleanin'."

"But ye're here to care for the babe," Bridgett reminded her.

"Och, 'tis nae all I can do. When I use the sling, I have two hands that can be workin'."

"Mayhap ye should ask Connor where he'd like ye to help," Bridgett suggested from the doorway. "I be certain he'd ken better than I."

Was her reluctance born out of truly not knowing what or where she could help, or something more? Onnleigh decided it best not to jump to conclusions. "Verra well, I shall ask him when he returns."

Bridgett smiled and left Onnleigh alone to tend to her babe.

AT NOONIN' time, Connor went to see Onnleigh and the babe. Now he stood in the shadows for a glimpse at the beautiful young red-headed woman. He found her lying on the cot with the babe sleeping next to her.

He thought it a most beautiful vision as feelings for this comely lass began to stir deep inside him. She was lovely; her auburn hair, twisted into a long braid, was tossed over her shoulder. Long, wispy strands had come loose and curled about her cheeks. He knew that were he to reach out and touch her sun-kissed skin, he'd find it as soft as silk. Full lips, pink as a spring rose, would be just as soft, but sweeter than any wine to taste.

He stood there, just at the shadow's edge, watching as her chest rose and fell, and wondered all manner of things. There was so much more to her than beautiful hair and bright eyes. For the most part, that something more was hidden just under the surface. Like a treasure secreted away for too many moons, waiting in graceful silence to be discovered.

How would his clan respond if he were to take her for a wife? This was not the first time he'd pondered that these past few weeks. Onnleigh was often in his thoughts. His admiration for her was growing by leaps and bounds on a daily basis.

Undoubtedly 'twould not go well for either of them, at least not now, for 'twas far too soon. Mayhap in time, after they had the chance to see what a truly fine young woman she was, her inner strength, her wit, and the way she loved her babe, they might warm to the idea.

There was something in her deep blue eyes, something he could not name, that spoke much about her character. Had she been given the same chances, the same amount of love and good upbringing as the other members of his clan, he imagined she'd be a powerful force, full of energy and light.

He did not believe the years of neglect at the hands of her father had doused that inner light completely. She was young yet, and he could not allow himself to think she was a lost cause. Nay, there was much hope for this young lass. All she needed was kindness and generosity, someone to help build her confidence, to show her she was so much more than a thief's daughter.

Just how much time it would take to accomplish such a feat was the burning question. The second question was who had fathered her babe. A sickening thought that made his stomach roil with disgust, was that mayhap her father had done more damage than simple neglect. 'Twas not unheard of, as much as the thought sickened him.

He couldn't press her for the information, not just yet. He had to build a trust between them first, before broaching such a horrific subject. He wondered then, would she ever be able to live a normal life if such an abomination were true? Would he be able to take her for wife if it turned out her father... No, he could not think about that.

All he could do at the moment was show her there were kind and decent people in this world.

ONNLEIGH WOKE to the sound of her daughter gurgling sweetly next to her. Guilt at having fallen asleep in the middle of the day assaulted her, albeit briefly. "Och, me sweetin'! How long have we been sleepin'?" she asked as she caressed Nola's cheek. "Twill nae get me in anyone's good graces to be a layabout."

With a wide yawn and a long, languid stretch, she sat up and looked about the room. "Did ye ever think we'd live so well?" she asked her babe. "I feel like a princess, sleepin' in a feather bed! Och! And the food. I ne'er kent to see so much of it in me lifetime."

Whether it was the large breakfast, the nap, the feather bed, or the warmth of the room, she couldn't rightly say. But whatever it was, she woke feeling refreshed and hopeful. For the first time in her life, she began to hum happily as she changed Nola, straightened the covers of her bed, and set about feeding her daughter.

"I dunnae wish anyone to think me lazy like me da. Och, child, I be so verra grateful that ye were nae forced to ken him. A mean drunkard he was. Ne'er a kind word e'er passed o'er his lips." Reckoning her babe would never remember this conversation, she felt at ease in telling her the truth about her lineage.

She looked about the small space with gratitude while Nola happily nursed at her breast. "All I e'er wanted was fer ye to have a good home, clean clothes, and enough to eat. Ye cannae see it now, and doubtful ye e'er will, but ye've been givin' a blessin' here, Nola. 'Tis a dream come true fer me as well.

"I wish I could do somethin' nice fer yer da. Nae yer real da, the lyin' cheat. But fer Connor. He will be the only da ye'll e'er ken, of that, I will make certain."

If she had a coin to her name, she'd give it to him. If she owned anything of value, she'd gladly hand it over in gratitude. But alas, she had neither coin nor possession. She might not be able to give him anything of true value, but she could *show* him how grateful she was.

As soon as Nola was finished, Onnleigh wrapped her in the sling and went below stairs, through the back door and into the kitchens in search of Louisa.

# CHAPTER 7

*A*fter returning to her bedchamber, she pulled off her good dress and changed into her skirt. Donning an apron Louisa had lent her, she pulled the cradle into Connor's room. Soon, two large men arrived with buckets, rags, and a broom. She thanked them kindly, offering up her warmest and most sincere smile. They cast each other quizzical looks before shrugging and leaving her to her task.

While Nola played in the cradle, Onnleigh scrubbed every inch of Connor's room. With the furs drawn away to let in the sunlight and fresh air, she swept out the fireplace, dusted the mantle, trunks, and tables. She put fresh linens on his bed and fluffed and arranged the pillows. By the time she was done, she was soaked in sweat, dust and grime.

Standing back, with hands on her hips, she smiled proudly at her good work. "That should show him," she whispered.

Moments later, she had wrapped Nola up again, picked up one of the buckets of dirty water and went below stairs to empty it.

As she crossed the gathering room, a young man came to offer his help. "Let me get that fer ye, lass," he said as he took the bucket from her hands.

"Thank ye kindly," she told him.

"I be Ronald, Connor's youngest brother," he explained.

"'Tis a pleasure to finally meet ye, Ronald," she said with a smile. "I have heard much about ye from yer brothers and Bridgett. I thank ye kindly fer yer help." Onnleigh noticed his cheeks grew dark when she mentioned Bridgett's name. She had to bite her lip to keep from giggling at him.

"Think not a thing of it, lass," he said. "Ye appear to have been quite busy this day."

"Aye, 'tis true. I have another bucket above stairs, and dirty linens that need a washin'," she told him.

"I'll send someone up fer those things, as ye appear to have yer hands full with the bairn," he said, inclining his head toward Nola.

"Her? She be no trouble at all, ye ken."

As they stood discussing the babe, Onnleigh caught sight of Bridgett, who was standing across the room with the oddest expression. "Bridgett," Onnleigh called out to her, "do ye have time to help me with somethin'?"

Ronald's countenance changed dramatically when he turned to see Bridgett walking towards them. Onnleigh did not catch the glances exchanged between the two, for her mind was elsewhere.

"How can I help ye?" Bridgett asked. Onnleigh thought her tone was off. Cold and distant, but she didn't understand why.

"It be of a most personal nature," she explained.

Ronald took the hint, bowed his head and left the two of them alone.

"I be in need of a bath," Onnleigh explained. "Could I get a dryin' cloth, soap and such? I would like to go to the loch and wash all this grime away."

"Why would ye go to the loch when there be a perfectly good bathin' house behind the kitchens?"

"What be a bathin' house?" Onnleigh asked.

"Connor had it built a few years ago, after he returned from Edinburgh. Before, we were either bathin' in the loch or in the kitchens.

The loch be too cold in winter and the kitchens be far too busy. Now we have a bathin' house."

Onnleigh had never heard of such a thing but was eager to see it for herself. "Thank ye, kindly, Bridgett. I shall go get me clean dress."

"Would ye like me to take Nola while ye bathe?"

The offer was too good to turn down. "That be awfully kind of ye. I promise, I'll nae tarry long."

Handing her daughter to Bridgett with much gratitude, Onnleigh raced back to her room to retrieve her blue dress and was soon off in search of the bathhouse.

IT WAS EASY TO FIND. As she stepped inside, a young maid of no more than ten and five was sitting on a little stool pulling on woolens. When she caught sight of Onnleigh, she tilted her blonde head to one side. "Who be ye?" she asked.

"Onnleigh. I be takin' care of Connor's babe," she told her nervously.

"I heard about ye," she replied with a smile. "I be Kate. Do ye need help?"

"'Twould be verra kind of ye," Onnleigh answered, much relieved to see a sincere smile from the young girl.

Kate led her toward a large pot with steaming water that sat over a healthy fire in the fireplace in the corner of the room. She chose the tub closest to the pot and began to scoop out buckets to fill it.

"There be soaps and dryin' cloths and such just there," Kate explained with a nod toward shelves on the other side of the room. Hesitantly, Onnleigh went to the shelves. Drying clothes filled the lower two shelves. The scents from the various jars of soap tickled at her nose. She'd been making her own soap since she was a little girl, but never had the luxury of adding scents to them. Picking up one jar at a time, she took tentative sniffs until she found one that she liked most. 'Twas a blend of marigolds and anemone, quite pleasing.

"Are ye certain I can use these?" Onnleigh asked.

"Aye, they be fer whoever needs them. Me mum makes the soaps herself, ye ken. If ye ever wish to have some to keep in yer room, just come see her. She'll sell them to ye at a fair price. But these are free for all."

Connor had mentioned she'd be paid for caring for Nola. Her heart felt lighter suddenly, with hope for a better future. In an instant, she decided one of her first purchases would be some of the fine soaps and later, when she'd saved up enough money, she could even afford a new dress.

"Yer bath be ready," Kate told her.

Onnleigh set the items on a stool by the tub. "Thank ye, kindly, Kate."

The girl smiled warmly again. "Call out if ye need anythin'," she said as she left Onnleigh alone.

ONCE KATE LEFT, Onnleigh quickly stripped out of her dirty clothes, undid her braid, and sank into the steamy water. She lay with her head against the edge of the tub, enjoying the luxuriously hot water and the way it instantly relaxed her. *Be it a sin to enjoy somethin' so simple?* she wondered. Remembering she'd promised Bridgett she would not tarry long, she dipped the washing cloth into the water and grabbed the jar of soap. She lathered and scrubbed every square inch of her body before setting about to wash her hair. The wonderful sensation of scrubbing her scalp clean felt so good, she washed it again.

Taking in a deep breath, she ducked her head under the water to rinse out the soap, running her fingers through the long strands, working out every last bit of soap. When she rose, breaking through the sudsy water, she let out a gasp of surprise, for she had company.

Three young women—only one of whom she had a vague recollection of ever seeing—were standing next to the tub. A bolt of fear stabbed her stomach. Sputtering, she wiped water from her eyes as she tried to steady her breathing.

"So ye be Onnleigh ingen Grueber," the one closest to her declared, her voice dripping with something ugly and untoward.

Onnleigh did not respond.

"Ye may try to wash the stench from ye, but 'twill do ye no good. Ye be as much a thief as yer da."

Anger rose in a flash. "I be no thief," she said through gritted teeth. "I've nae stolen anythin'."

The brunette quirked a pretty brow. "Ye've stolen Ronald from Bridgett and Connor from me," she said pointedly. "How many men does one whore need?"

Confusion blended with anger. "I only met Ronald a few moments ago. I've nae stolen him from anyone. And Connor—"

"Connor be *mine*, ye stupid wench! Ye move in here and turn his head with yer red hair and charms and now he says he'll nae marry me as we planned."

*Margaret.* This had to be Helen's daughter, for she was just as haughty, just as spiteful. None of what she said was true. Onnleigh was no thief, no whore, and to be called such made her all the more angry. "I only be here to care for his babe," she said.

"His babe? That bastard child is nae Connor's and never will be. And ye? Ye will never be anything more than a thief and whore. Everyone kens it. We dunnae want ye here, *thief.* Leave while ye still have a chance."

'Twas more than an idle threat in the undertone of her words. 'Twas a promise of things to come, should she decide to stay. Why Margaret was convinced she'd stolen anything was a mystery to her. Onnleigh'd only just met Ronald, and Connor was nothing more than her chief. Nay, he was more than that. He was the man who had given her a chance. *Show them what a kind young woman ye are*, he'd said. She heard his words as clearly as if he were standing beside her now.

From somewhere deep within, she found the courage to stand up to this brown-haired young woman. *I'll be kind, but I'll also be strong. I be right tired of people thinkin' they can call me names and treat me poorly.* "I'll nae leave unless Connor tells me to."

Margaret stood to her full height, eyes glaring angrily with a depth of malice Onnleigh had never before seen. "Ye've been warned. Leave of your own accord or I'll make it so the clan runs ye out like the thief I ken ye to be."

Margaret turned to look at the two young women who'd come with her. At her sharp nod, they scurried to the shelves and scooped up all the drying cloths, hurrying from the bathhouse. Margaret picked up Onnleigh's clothing and the drying cloth she had set on the stool earlier. "Enjoy yer bath," she said as she sashayed out of the room.

"Bring back me clothes!" Onnleigh cried out.

Margaret stopped and turned to look back. "These?" she asked spitefully. "I would nae even put them in the rag bin. Lord only kens what vermin and filth they be covered in." And with that, she left an angry, stunned Onnleigh in a bath full of tepid water.

She had tried calling out for Kate, the young woman who had helped her, but the lass never appeared. Onnleigh sat in the tub, the water growing colder, her anger hotter with each passing moment.

*What right does she have to do this to me?* Onnleigh thought to herself. *I've ne'er done a thing to her. To anyone.*

The longer she sat, the more furious she became.

Before long, she was too angry to think clearly enough to make any kind of wise decision. Finally, she shot to her feet and stepped out of the tub. There was not a drying cloth to be found. Angrily, she stomped through the place, hunting for something with which to cover herself. Thankfully, no one else was about. A quick search led her to one damp drying cloth that had fallen to the floor between two tubs.

'Twas barely big enough to cover breasts and parts not meant to be seen by anyone, but 'twould do for now. In a fury, she went off in search of Margaret.

ANGRILY, she stomped across the cold, damp earth, through muddy spots, calling out Margaret's name as she went. Unable to find her out-of-doors, she flung open the door to the kitchens, surprising all within. The drying cloth did little to cover everything.

"Have ye seen the one called Margaret?" she demanded. "Helen's daughter?"

Rapid shakes of multiple heads were the only answer she received. Slamming the door shut, she crossed the small space between kitchen and keep, flung open the door and headed inside.

There, in the middle of the crowded gathering room, was Margaret and her two friends, huddled together, giggling, no doubt at Onnleigh's expense.

With hands clenched into tight fists, angry as a bull, she went to them. "Where. Are. My. Clothes." Her words were clipped, filled with a lifetime of frustration and anger.

Margaret feigned ignorance. "Yer clothes? I fear I dunnae ken what ye mean."

So angry her hands and legs were trembling, Onnleigh took one step forward. "Ye ken *exactly* what I mean. Where are me clothes?"

"Again, I tell ye I dunnae what ye mean," Margaret said dismissively. "Mayhap a thief took them?"

"Ye are a mean, spiteful, foul woman!" Onnleigh growled. "'Tis nae wonder none wants ye as a wife. Now give me back me clothes."

"I'd rather be mean and spiteful than a thief or a whore," Margaret said, leaning in so only Onnleigh could hear clearly.

In a fury of pent up anger, Onnleigh drew back her hand and slapped Margaret across the face. 'Twas the first time in her life she'd ever struck another living thing.

Before Margaret could retaliate, Ronald appeared from somewhere, wrapped his arms around her waist and pulled her away. Someone was doing the same to Onnleigh.

"Ye be a wretched whore and nothin' more!" Margaret shouted as her arms flailed out in an attempt to reach her foe.

"Ye're nothin' but a mean and hateful person!" Onnleigh shouted back. "I've ne'er done a thing to ye, yet ye call me names and accuse me of doin' things I've ne'er done!"

Connor's deep voice boomed and echoed off the walls. "Stop!"

It had been he who grabbed her and pulled her away from Margaret. He startled Onnleigh into silence, but Margaret continued with her accusations and hate-filled words.

"Will someone please tell me what the bloody hell is goin' on?" Connor shouted.

"She took me clothes," Onnleigh told him over her shoulder.

"I did no such thing!"

"Ye did! While I was bathin', ye came in and accused me of stealin' Ronald from Bridgett and Connor from ye." Her heart began to hurt, her anger subsiding, only to be replaced with humiliation and shame.

"Bah! Ye lie! Ye're a thief and a liar as well as a whore!"

Tears stung at Onnleigh's eyes, fury and humiliation blending into a very ugly combination. "'Tis nae true," she said, her voice hoarse and scratchy.

"Ronald, take Margaret to me study and dunnae allow her to leave," Connor ordered as he set Onnleigh on her feet. Taking her hand, he said, "Come with me."

He led her above stairs and into her room. Bridgett was sitting in a chair with Nola in her arms. Her eyes opened in surprise when she saw Connor pulling Onnleigh inside.

"Leave us," he told her. "Wait fer me in the hall with Nola," Connor ordered. She hurried from the room without question.

Onnleigh could sense he was trying to keep his temper in check. She slumped into the chair, drawing the damp drying cloth around her shoulders. *Margaret was right. They'll all be ready to hang me now. And Connor will be the one to put the noose around me neck.*

"Get dressed," he told her, his tone of voice filled with frustration.

"I cannae," she told him, her face burning with humiliation. *Why did ye let her do that to ye?*

"Why nae?" he asked as he stood next to her with his arms crossed over his chest.

"Because Margaret took me clothes."

He stood in silence for a long while. "Why would she do that?"

Onnleigh could not yet find the strength to look at him. "I told ye below stairs why."

"Tell me again," he said, his voice not sounding nearly as angry as before.

She took in a deep breath, fighting back the urge to cry. "I was in the bathin' house. She came in and accused me of stealing Ronald from Bridgett even though I'd only just met him. He offered to carry the buckets fer me. I swear, 'twas the first time I e'er saw him."

"Buckets?" he asked.

She sniffed, wiped her eyes on the edge of the drying cloth. "I cleaned yer room this afternoon."

A length of silence passed before he asked, "Why did ye do that?'

Shrugging her shoulders as if the why of it was not important, she remained silent.

He pulled up a chair and sat beside her. "Onnleigh, why did ye clean me room?"

"It needed a good cleanin'," she told him. 'Twas not necessarily a full lie, only a half-truth.

"Was there another reason?"

She didn't understand why 'twas so important to him. Mayhap he only wanted to know so he'd have all the facts before he hung her or made her leave. Her heart felt heavy, her soul utterly unworthy. "I wanted to do somethin' nice fer ye," she murmured softly. "I could nae give ye anythin' to show me thanks. Cleanin' yer room seemed the least I could do."

He swallowed hard. "To thank me fer what?"

Finally, she allowed herself the chance to look at him full on. He didn't appear nearly as angry as she had expected. Instead, there was a warmth in his eyes, that look of kind regard she was growing far too fond of. "Fer bein' so kind when no one else was. Fer givin' me a chance. Fer lovin' Nola as if she were yer own. Fer standin' up to Helen.." *Fer nae lookin' at me as if I were as wretched and undeserving as Margaret declared.*

He let out a long breath through his nostrils. "Tell me what happened in the bath house."

"Margaret and her friends came in. She accused me of stealin' Ronald from Bridgett…" she let her words trail off, afraid to admit to the rest.

"And?"

Och, he was a persistent man. She took another steadying breath before going on. "She said I stole ye from her," she said before quickly adding, "I tried to tell her 'twas nae true!" *A man like ye would ne'er be wantin' a thing like me.*

Another frustrated sigh passed over his lips. "I have never been interested in Margaret. 'Tis in her mind and her mum's that I should marry her, but nothin' could be further from me mind." He looked at her for a long time before pushing himself to his feet. "I be sorry they did that to ye, lass. Verra sorry."

He was apologizing to her for something he had not done. She looked at him in wonder and awe.

"Then she took yer clothes?"

Too stunned to speak, she could only offer a nod.

His anger returned, but now she knew 'twas not directed at her. "I will be puttin' an end to this once and fer all, lass. Ye stay here. I'll see to it that ye have a dress to wear. Put on yer chemise before ye catch yer death." He set about lighting a fire in the brazier.

Though she did not want to admit it aloud, she had to. "I do nae have a chemise."

He looked up from the brazier. "She took that as well?"

Onnleigh shook her head. "Nae, I mean, I do nae have a chemise. I use me tunic as such. She took it along with me dress. All I have left is me brown skirt. I have naught else." Humiliation burned her cheeks a deep red.

'Twas not pity she saw staring back at her, but something else she could not identify.

"I'll make sure ye have all ye need, lass," he told her warmly.

Moments later, a nice fire was burning in the brazier. He went to her bed, withdrew the fine wool blanket and wrapped it around her shoulders. "I'll return as soon as I can. Stay here and wait fer me."

There was nothing else she could say, but a thousand things she wished she could put to voice.

Giving her a pat on the shoulder and a look filled with promises, he smiled before quitting the room.

~

"TELL me why Margaret would accuse Onnleigh of takin' Ronald from ye?" Connor asked, his arms crossed over his broad chest as he stared down at Bridgett. "And tell me the truth."

Bridgett looked as fearful as she did contrite. She stammered, tripping over her own tongue before she could finally answer clearly. "I saw them talkin' below stairs. It made me angry. She's so pretty, ye ken."

*Aye, I ken.*

"I did nae think Margaret would do such a cruel thing," she said, hoping that excuse would gain her some leniency.

"Ye've known Margaret all yer life. What made ye think she'd be kind about it—or anythin' else?"

With her gaze on her boots, she did not immediately answer.

"Onnleigh has nae stolen Ronald from ye. But as far as I see it, Ronald be nae yers, fer ye haven't told him how ye feel. If ye wish to make him yers, ye must tell him. Quit hidin' behind yer shyness and declare yer love for him. Elst I'll be forced to find him a wife, and ye'll nae be it."

She lifted her head so fast he was surprised she didn't snap her own neck. She dared not voice any objections, for she knew he'd make good on his promise.

"Take Nola to Onnleigh and apologize to her. Then ye go and find a pretty dress for her, as well as a chemise, anythin' else she might need."

"I be so sorry, Connor," she told him.

"Do nae tell me. Tell Onnleigh," he said before leaving her alone in the hallway.

~

IT HAD NOT TAKEN LONG for word about Onnleigh and Margaret's argument to spread throughout the clan. By the time Connor made his way to the study, Helen was waiting for him. Braigh and Ronald followed behind him, more likely than not to keep their brother from strangling Margaret or Helen or both.

With protective arms wrapped around her none-too-innocent daughter, Helen instantly began to tell him what she thought.

"She slapped me poor daughter in front of everyone!" she screamed as he made his way to his desk. "Do ye nae see how injured me Margaret is? Please tell me ye have thrown that wretched creature into the dungeon!"

Connor rolled his eyes, not believing for an instant that Margaret was as severely upset as her mother wanted him to believe. "Should I also throw yer daughter into the dungeon fer stealin'?"

Margaret stared at him, aghast that he could even think such a thing. "Margaret? She's never stolen a thing in her life!"

"She stole Onnleigh's clothes and tossed them in a fire," he told her. He had learned that bit of information from Ronald only moments before stepping into the office. "That is stealin'."

Margaret sniffed and turned away from her mother's breast. "I thought they were rags," she beseeched him. "I did nae ken they were her clothes."

"Then ye would nae mind givin' her a few of yer dresses to make up fer yer mistake?" the laird asked with a smile.

Both women were appalled by the idea. "Nay!" Margaret exclaimed. "I'll nae part with any of me things, least of all to *her!*"

"There, there, my child," Helen said as she patted Margaret's hand. "'Twas an honest mistake. I've seen what the girl calls clothes. None can hold ye responsible fer mistakin' them fer rags."

"I can," Connor told them. "And I do."

Helen glowered at him with hate. "That *thief*, that *filthy* creature slapped me daughter in front of one and all. I'll nae stand idly by while ye do nothin'!"

Connor's smile faded instantly. "She is nae a thief nor filthy creature. She be a kind, sweet lass, and ye'll never call her anything but her given name ever again."

"Until a fortnight ago, ye dinnae even ken who she was," Helen told him. "She's bewitched ye. Turned ye away from me Margaret. Turned yer head, she has. She be a witch!"

To be accused as a witch was worse than any other insult and could spell a death sentence if she were able to convince enough of his clanspeople 'twas the truth. He stood to his full height, spread his palms on top of his desk and leaned forward. "Hear me and hear me well," he said in a low, firm voice, "Onnleigh be no witch nor thief nor anythin' else ye've accused her of this day. Hear this as well, and make no mistake in me words. I will never, *ever* marry Margaret. She could be the last woman on God's earth and I still would nae marry her."

Two sets of stunned eyes stared back at him. "How can ye say that?" Helen asked. "After all Margaret has done fer ye."

He quirked a brow. "All Margaret has done fer me? Please, pray tell, begin listin' all the wonderful, kind things she's done fer me."

"She's kept herself fer ye," Helen began.

"And?" Connor challenged.

"And she's loved ye and offered to be yer wife since me sweet Maire died."

"Those be nae kind gestures but a woman hopin' fer more than she'll ever have," Braigh offered from near the fireplace.

Helen shot an angry glance toward him before turning back to Connor. "Margaret has—"

Connor raised his hand to silence her. "Has Margaret done anythin' but declare she'll marry me?"

Helen was at a loss for words. "She loves ye."

Connor gave a long, slow shake of his head. "Nay, she does nae love me. She loves the idea of being the chief's wife and chatelaine of the keep. But she does nae love me. We will stop this charade at once. I will nae marry her. Nae now, nae ever."

Margaret looked to her mother, her face drawn into a knot of anger and pain. "'Tis all her fault! She's turned him against me!"

Connor slammed his fist down hard onto his desk. "No one has turned me against ye! I was never yers to begin with!" He took in a deep breath before going on. "I will nae repeat what I've told ye. The two of ye shall get the notion of a marriage betwixt us out of yer minds, once and for all. And ye will stay clear of Onnleigh, do ye understand? No more hateful accusations, no more name callin', no more stealin' her clothes. I do nae want either one of ye anywhere near her. Or me fer that matter."

He stood tall with his shoulders back. "Do ye understand me?"

Although they nodded in confirmation, deep down, Connor knew he was not done hearing from these two, cold-hearted women. And neither was Onnleigh.

# CHAPTER 8

*B*ridgett had done her best to apologize to Onnleigh, as well as to explain why she'd been so jealous.

"I've done everythin' I can think of to get Ronald to look me way. I've loved that man since I was seven summers. I was jealous and angry that he should be smilin' at ye as he was, with yer pretty red hair and yer face."

Onnleigh stared in abject confusion. "Me face?" she asked, uncertain what her face had to do with anything.

"Och, Onnleigh! Ye're beautiful! I cannae compete with ye."

Closing her eyes, she shook her head as if that would bring come clarity to the situation. "Ye're daft. Ye be the beautiful one, Bridgett, nae me. I could nae more turn a man's head than I could fly."

Although Darwud had often bespoke how beautiful he found her, she knew 'twas all a lie. Empty words she had foolishly allowed herself to believe. She was as common as a blade of Highland grass.

"But ye are," Bridgett argued further. "I ken ye dunnae believe it, but ye are. 'Twas why I grew so jealous. 'Twas a mean and spiteful thing to tell Margaret. I should have known she'd be cruel, but I was so upset and fearful that I'd lose Ronald to ye that I was nae right in me own head."

Though she did not believe she was beautiful as Bridgett was suggesting, she could understand her fear. She'd been fearful as well an hour ago when she thought Connor was going to make her leave the clan. Fear could make a person do things they might not otherwise do. Such as giving up her own babe.

"Will ye forgive me?" Bridgett asked pitifully.

Onnleigh let out a long sigh. "Aye, I forgive ye. But only if ye promise to come to me first if I e'er do anythin' to upset ye. Ken me heart and ken that I'd ne'er intentionally bring ye an ounce of pain."

Bridgett's shoulders relaxed in relief. "Thank ye, Onnleigh!" she exclaimed as she wrapped her arms around her and hugged tightly.

Unaccustomed to physical displays of emotion or affection, Onnleigh stood rigid for a long moment. The last person who had hugged her had been her mum. In her mind, what she'd done with Darwud on the banks of the stream that day last year did not count. A long moment passed before she felt comfortable enough to return the hug.

"I swear, I'll make it up to ye someday," Bridgett said as she pulled away and smiled.

"As long as ye promise to come to me first if I've done somethin' wrong, we shall be friends fer a long while."

Bridgett seemed pleased with her answer. "I promise, I shall. Now wait here fer a moment, I shall be back shortly."

Onnleigh returned to her chair by the fire, still wrapped in the drying cloth and blanket. Quietly, she prayed that Margaret would confess soon so that her clothes would be returned to her.

A moment later, Bridgett returned with something draped over her arms. "Connor bade me get ye a dress and chemise. I also found ye some warm woolens and a plaid."

Surprised, Onnleigh stared up at her. "I dunnae understand," she said. "All I need is me clothes to be returned. I cannae afford to buy anythin' yet. I've nae been paid me wages."

Bridgett rolled her eyes as she set the articles on the bed. "Ye dunnae have to purchase these. They be a gift from me to ye. The gown might be a bit tight in the bodice, but I think we can manage."

Onnleigh stood slowly and stared at the dress Bridgett was holding up for her inspection. 'Twas a beautiful woolen gown, woven in shades of purple and blue the color of the midnight sky. The sleeves were long, the edges trimmed in dark shades of purple like the rest of the dress. 'Twas a color that reminded her of that late hour of the night when the moon did not shine and the sun was just threatening to come up in the east. Inky indigo and purple, dark with a promise of a new day to come.

'Twas a magnificent gown. One she felt wholly unworthy of wearing.

"Do ye like it?" Bridgett asked hopefully

"I cannae wear such a nice gown," Onnleigh told her breathlessly. Her fingers itched to reach out and touch it, certain 'twas as soft and luxurious as it appeared.

"Och! Dunnae be silly. 'Tis one of me auld gowns me mum made fer me at least three years ago. I want ye to have it. The chemise and woolens too."

Aside from Connor giving her food to eat, a warm bed to sleep in, and Nola a future, the dress, the clothes, were the single nicest thing anyone had ever done for her. Those tears she'd been fighting came tumbling down her cheeks. There was naught she could do to stop them.

Attempting to choke them back, she thanked Bridgett repeatedly.

"Think nothin' of it," Bridgett said happily. "'Tis the least I can do."

*Nae,* she thought to herself. *Ye could have done less. Ye could have nae admitted yer mistake. Ye could have turned away from me, to let me suffer alone.*

CONNOR HAD RETURNED to Onnleigh with the intention of informing her that he had warned Helen and Margaret to leave her be.

But when he saw her sitting on the stool, combing her hair out with an old comb, wearing a most lovely indigo dress, those thoughts slipped his mind.

She stole his very breath away.

Her smile, so honest and genuine, asking nothing from him but kindness, made his knees quake.

The way the candlelight and flames from the brazier danced and flickered across her skin, her auburn hair, casting her in a near ethereal glow, was mesmerizing. He stood for the longest time, drinking her in as if he were a man whose thirst could not be quenched with anything earthly.

"What be the matter?" she asked. When he did not respond, she set the comb aside, her smile replaced with a look of great concern. "Have I done somethin' wrong?"

"Nay, lass," he answered, his throat having turned mysteriously dry.

Tilting her head to one side, she continued to look at him, curious and worried all at once. A thought suddenly occurred to her; mayhap he thought she'd stolen the dress. "I dinnae take it," she began to explain quickly. "Bridgett gave it to me. The chemise and the woolens too. Ye can ask her yerself—"

He held up a hand. "I ken she did, lass. I ken ye'd nae take anythin' that dinnae belong to ye."

Relieved, she let her shoulders relax and expelled a long breath. "I ne'er owned such a fine thing before. I tried to tell her I dinnae need anythin' so pretty, but she'd nae listen."

"I'm glad she dinnae," he told her in a soft, warm voice. "Ye look verra beautiful in it."

She'd have been far less surprised had he told her she'd sprouted horns atop her head. "Don't be daft," she told him dismissively. As much as she would have liked to believe him, she knew 'twas dangerous to do so. Wanting to keep her mind from wandering to places it should not, she picked up her comb again.

"I be nae daft," he told her as he crossed his arms over his chest.

Pretending to ignore him, she combed her hair and focused her attention on the brazier.

"I came to tell ye that I spoke with Helen and Margaret. I wish I could tell ye they'd nae be botherin' ye again, but I fear 'twould be a lie," he said as he took the chair next to her.

"Helen has nae e'er liked me," she told him.

He raised a curious brow. "Ye've known her long then?"

"Aye, I ken her."

Politely, he asked for further explanation.

"Me mum passed when I was five, ye ken. Grueber, he was nae verra good at carin' for a wee one. He was nae good at anythin' but drinkin' and takin' that which didnae belong to him. I learned early on to care fer meself, fer no one else was goin' to. When I was nine, we came to the village. There was a group of children playin' hide and find but they wouldna let me play. 'Twas all right, fer they ne'er let me play and I was used to it. Still, I watched from a distance, wishin' fer all the world they'd let me in, but as usual, they did nae. Later, one of the mum's came and gave them all sweet cakes. All but me. I was terrible hungry, I was. Ye could hear me stomach a growlin' clear to Loch Moy, I imagine. The children, they kent I was hungry, but they'd nae share those sweet cakes. One of the boys, Thomas be his name, he said, 'I ken ye're hungry Onnleigh. Ye can have some leeks from that garden o'er there. They will nae mind.'"

Connor watched her closely as she told the story. His heart broke at the telling.

Onnleigh laid the comb on her lap and took a deep breath. "Even at nine summers, I kent well what me da was. But me hunger was powerful strong that day. I truly believed Thomas was bein' kind, ye ken. Now, mind ye, I dunnae like leeks. But when ye're hungry, ye'll eat just about anythin'. So I tiptoed into that wee garden and I took three leeks. I didnae even get a chance to eat them, fer once Helen saw me there, she came flyin' out o' her cottage like her hair was on fire. She was a yellin' and callin' me thief. I tried to explain, but she would nae listen, so angry she was. Beat me backside raw all the way from her cottage to the gate. That be how I got this scar." She leaned forward and pointed to a tiny scar that ran from her lip to her nostril.

"I tripped, ye see, and fell face first onto a verra sharp rock. I learned that day ne'er to take anythin' from anyone, and the only person I could rely on in this world was meself." She sat back and began rubbing her fingers across her comb. "I've stayed away from the keep and the people e'er since. That was more 'n ten years ago."

His contempt toward Helen turned to sheer, unadulterated hatred. How one being could treat another, especially someone so young, with such malice, such an unkind heart, was baffling.

"So ye see, Helen does nae like me much, and in truth, I do nae care much fer her," she admitted. "But I be no thief. I be no whore or wretched creature like they think me."

"I ken ye be none of those things," he told her. "I be sorry ye had to endure such sufferin'."

She looked up at him with a wan smile. "Please, do nae start pityin' me now."

"'Tis nae pity, Onnleigh. This I promise ye. Had I kent what you had gone through—"

"What would ye have done? Stopped them? Ye were but a lad, and if memory serves me correctly, ye were nae even here at the time. Ye were off fosterin'."

"I would have told me da. He could have stopped them," he told her with so much conviction that Onnleigh almost believed him.

She took in a deep breath. "Enough of talkin' about what cannae be undone." And what was painful to recall.

"I want to know ye better, Onnleigh. I want to know everythin' about ye." The words were out and there was naught he could do to pull them back. He realized then that, in truth, he didn't wish to unsay them.

"Me?" she asked with a good measure of disbelief. "Ye're daft."

"Nae, I be nae daft, no matter how often ye call me so. I do wish to ken ye better."

She laughed derisively. "The last time a man told me that I ended up—" She stopped herself short before she said anything she could not undo.

Connor had a feeling he knew what she was going to say, but he left it alone. She would tell him someday, when she was ready. "Onnleigh, I think ye be a fine young woman."

She eyed him suspiciously for a moment. Dare she believe him?
"'Tis true lass. I'd never tell ye false."

When she looked into those bright eyes of his, she saw no deceit, no ulterior motives. That inner voice, the one she hadn't listened to a year ago when she should have, was eerily quiet.

He smiled warmly and took her hands in his. "I ken ye've nae had an easy way of things. I ken ye nae be used to anyone bein' kind or generous. But I need ye to believe in me, to ken what be in me heart."

Her bright blue eyes were brimming with tears she was trying gallantly to keep at bay.

"When I look at ye, I do nae see a young woman raised poor. I see a verra strong woman with a light inside her so bright 'tis nearly blindin'. I see a beautiful, kind young woman who, if given a chance, could rise above all she has endured and become a fine, fine woman."

She looked away, not wanting him to see her fear, her doubts, all her worries.

"I do nae ken how it has happened, these feelin's I have fer ye. When I first laid eyes upon ye, somethin' happened to me heart. 'Twas as if ye were someone I'd been waitin' fer me entire life.

"Onnleigh, I wish to marry ye."

HE WASN'T TELLING her these things in order to convince her to lift her skirts. There was too much sincerity in his voice, too much adoration in his eyes. Still, doubts lingered. Not that tiny voice of warning, but one born of self-doubt, years of feeling unworthy of affection or kindness. How could anyone, especially the chief of her clan, possess such feelings toward the likes of her?

"Ye cannae say such things, Connor," she told him, fighting back the urge to run fast and far and never look back.

"Why? Why can I nae say what be in me heart?"

Swallowing hard, she replied, "Ye need a better woman than me. A woman the clan can admire. Ye need someone who kens how to read, write, and cipher. A woman who kens how to run a keep. I cannae do any of those things. I'd only bring ye shame."

He scowled at her. "Never say that," he said firmly. "Ye could never bring me shame. I'd be very proud to call ye wife."

One errant tear escaped and trailed down her cheek. "Ye say that now, but what of yer clan? Are ye prepared fer them to hate ye fer tossin' o'er one of yer own fer me?"

He took in a deep, cleansing breath. "Onnleigh, I be nae tossin' anyone aside. There be no one else I want but ye. And the clan? They be yer clan as well as mine."

Shaking her head, she had to disagree. "Ye ken what Helen and Margaret think of me. Do ye really believe they be the only two who think that?"

"I dunnae care what anyone thinks. I ken that once they see ye as I see ye, they'll soon be changin' their minds. Besides, we already have allies in me brothers, in Bridgett, and even in Louisa. She's quite fond of ye, ye ken, and that, dear Onnleigh, is nae an easy thing to accomplish."

With the pads of his thumbs, he brushed tears from her cheeks. "Please, Onnleigh, say ye'll marry me."

"I dunnae understand," she told him through free-flowing tears.

"Dunnae understand what?" he asked, wiping away more of those tears.

"How could ye have feelin's fer me?"

"I dunnae understand it meself. All I ken is what is in me heart. And me heart says 'tis hopeless to deny these feelin's. I want ye to be me wife."

She thought back to the day she'd made her wish at the old well. She had not wished for anything for herself that day, only for her babe. A warm, safe home, with parents who would cherish her, provide for her.

Now, she was sitting beside Connor MacCallen, the chief of their clan, and he was asking for her hand. *Hers.* The thief's daughter.

"Are ye sure 'tis nae pity that makes ye want me?"

He looked aghast at the idea. "Nae, I feel no pity for ye, lass, only admiration."

One look in his eyes was all she needed. He was nae telling her these things just to get under her skirt. These weren't empty, false words, but words from his heart. Until that moment, she hadn't allowed herself to think him anything more than her chief. A handsome and kind man, to be certain. But a husband?

Again, her thoughts turned back to the wish. Was it possible that whoever 'twas who made wishes come true had looked deep into her heart and seen the truth? Aye, she wanted a family for Nola, but she also wanted more that she daren't voice or give a moment's thought to; she wanted a husband. Someone who would be kind to her, a man she could be proud of, someone who would protect her. Connor would be and do all those things, and more. In her heart of hearts, she knew he'd cherish her as well.

Onnleigh pushed aside all the doubts, the worries, the fear, and let her heart fly freely for the first time in an age.

"Aye, Connor MacCallen. I shall marry ye."

HE COULD NOT HAVE BEEN MORE happy were he just made King of Scotia. Wrapping his arms around her waist, he picked her up and twirled her about the room. "Ye've made me a verra happy man, Onnleigh! A verra happy man!"

'Twas a dream come true for Onnleigh ingen Grueber as well.

"I'll have the banns posted on the morrow, if that be alright with ye? We can marry in six weeks?" he said, his voice full of hope, his smile so big and bright there was no need for candles.

"Aye, ye can post them. And aye, I'll marry ye in six weeks," she said, allowing her heart to fill with more joy and happiness than she'd ever felt.

In such a short time they would marry, become a family. With Connor already claiming Nola as his own, Onnleigh would be allowed to call herself mother, and none would be the wiser nor question it.

In six weeks, they would begin a life together as husband and wife.

From her cradle, Nola gurgled, bringing Onnleigh back to reality.

*Nola. How do I tell him about Nola?*

She did not want to begin a marriage with such a secret looming over her head. Besides, come the wedding night, he would most assuredly discover her missing maidenhead. A part of her wanted to wait before telling him, for fear he'd change his mind. But the honest part of her knew that to keep such a secret would be the same as lying. She could only pray that he would neither change his mind nor become so enraged he'd ask her to leave.

"Connor, I need to tell ye somethin', somethin' verra important," she said as she broke their embrace and stepped away.

Cocking his head slightly, he looked at her with curiosity. "What is it?"

It took a few deep breaths and twisting of her fingers to muster the courage to spit it all out. She told him everything, from the first day Darwud had appeared on her doorstep, to the last day she had seen him. Out of fear and humiliation, she left out a few significant pieces of information—such as Darwud's identity and that he had slapped her.

To his credit, Connor listened thoughtfully as she paced the floor, purging the secret, or as much of it as she could. Her voice trembled with anger at times, and grew soft when she felt the surge of humiliation washing over her again. "I be nae a whore," she told him. "But 'twas the first time in an age anyone had shown me a kindness or given me a sweet word."

When she was finished, she turned to face him, looking directly into his eyes, certain she would find anger or resentment in them. Instead, she found only acceptance.

"Who is he?" he asked, his calm voice belying his anger.

Twisting her fingers together, she asked, "Is nae tellin' ye the same as lyin'?"

He let loose a deep, frustrated breath. "Why do ye nae want me to know?"

"I worry that if he finds out, he'll try to take her from me," she answered in a low, worried voice. "I tried once to give her away, but could nae do it. I love her too much, Connor. I ken now that I cannae live without her."

He came to her then and wrapped his arms around her protectively. "He will never take our daughter from us. I do nae care who sired her, she still be mine. Ours." He kissed the top of her head as she melted into him.

"Ye still want me?" she asked in disbelief.

Gently, he pushed her away to look into her eyes. "Of course I still want ye as me wife. What happened in the past does nae change that."

Relief washed over her, melting her heart as she looked into those bright eyes of his. A long, silent moment stretched on, as unspoken promises passed between them.

With tender fingers, he lifted her chin, bent low and pressed his lips to hers. A warm, tickling sensation began deep in her stomach, something she could not remember feeling when Darwud had kissed her. Nay, this was not the same desperate sensation; 'twas warm, sweet, wondrous. There was a sense of safety in his touch, a promise that he'd never hurt her and would lay down his own life to protect her.

She melted into him, slowly returning the kiss with the same passion and promises.

After long moments, he pulled away reluctantly, only so his passion would not overwhelm him. He'd not take her to his bed until they were good and properly wed. But that did not mean he'd not think about that moment, or be tempted, especially when he saw her blue eyes filled with desire and passion of her own.

She cleared her throat once, then again. "Can we post banns for *three* weeks instead of six?"

Throwing his head back, he laughed heartily. "Aye lass, we can if ye wish."

"I do," she said as she pressed her head against his chest.

In three weeks they would be married. And never again would anyone look upon her with pity or shame or mistrust. Nay, she'd never again be called *the thief's daughter.* Instead, she would be Onnleigh, wife of Connor, the chief of Clan MacCallen.

# CHAPTER 9

*A*fter a lengthy discussion, Connor and Onnleigh decided 'twould be best to wait until after the Yuletide before making their engagement public. Onnleigh did not mind, for she was still fighting hard to get the clan to accept her. Knowing it was going to be a long, hard-fought battle, waiting seemed the most logical course of action.

'Twas Yuletide eve and the keep was bustling with excitement. Children ran and played within the walls. Some took sweet cakes when they thought no one was looking, though the evidence was quite clearly left behind on their faces and fingers.

Joyful music filled the air as the Yule log was placed upon the hearth with great ceremony. Between the telling of stories and pulling children away from the sweet cakes, singing and gaiety, the keep was as alive as Connor could ever remember it being.

During all this, Onnleigh kept to the corner of the room while she quietly observed the festivities as she held Nola close. Once, Louisa brought a flagon of goat's milk for the babe, not knowing 'twasn't necessary. Onnleigh thanked her before disappearing above stairs under the guise of needing to change the babe.

'Twas to Connor's great relief when she returned not long after, even if she did go back to the corner. He hoped that someday soon she would feel far more comfortable amongst their people. For now, all he could do was set a good example to the others.

Before they made an official announcement to his clan or posted banns or began making plans for their wedding ceremony, there was one thing Connor felt compelled to do. 'Twas silly of course, for he still didn't fully believe in wishes. But his life had changed dramatically in the weeks since visiting the well. Mayhap there was something to be said for wishes after all.

Pulling Louisa aside, he asked for her assistance. "Could ye take care of Nola for a little while? There be somethin' Onnleigh and I need to do."

The woman glanced first at Onnleigh, then back to her chief. A knowing smile broke out on her face. "Should I be plannin' fer a weddin'?" she asked.

The color drained from Connor's face. "Louisa, I beg ye nae to say a word to anyone just yet."

She gave him a warm pat on the arm. "Do nae fash over it, Connor. I'll be keepin' it to meself."

He studied her closely for a long moment before asking, "How did ye immediately jump to that conclusion?"

"Och, I've kent ye since the day ye were born. Ye sometimes wear yer heart on yer sleeve. I see how ye've been lookin' at her."

"And ye will nae be against it?"

"Me?" she asked with much surprise. "Now when have I ever been against ye?"

With a shrug and a shake of his head, he said, "I cannae remember." 'Twas true he'd known her his entire life. Louisa, along with his grandmother, were the two constants in his life, and Louisa had always been his champion.

"Aye. Now, were ye to be listenin' to Helen and ready to announce yer betrothal to Margaret? Why I'd be packin' me things and leavin' ye before sun-up, lettin' ye all starve to death."

He could not resist smiling or feigning hurt. "Ye'd leave me? I fear I could nae survive without ye."

She rolled her eyes. "And do nae ye ever forget it, laddie."

He gave her a warm hug and thanked her kindly. Stepping away, he smiled thoughtfully. "I be verra glad to have ye as me ally, Louisa. I hope ye'll be Onnleigh's as well."

She turned her attention to Onnleigh for a long moment. "I remember when she was born too. Och, such a pretty babe she was. As beautiful as her mum."

"I fear I do nae remember much of her mum and da, nor Onnleigh."

"She was a good woman. Someday, I shall tell ye how she came to be married to Grueber, fer 'twill take a long while and a wee bit of whisky to tell it."

Although his interest was piqued, the sun would soon be setting, and his time running short. "I look forward to it. Now, let us go and see if we can't pry that babe out of her hands."

It had taken some work on Connor's part to convince his betrothed the babe would be fine in the capable hands of their cook, and to get Onnleigh headed toward the stables.

"Where be we goin'?" she asked as they crossed the yard.

"I wish ye to ride with me," he told her as he led the way.

"Ride what?" she asked with a furrowed brow.

He chuckled softly. "Me horse."

She came to an abrupt halt. "I've ne'er been on one before."

"Do nae worry it, lass. Ye'll be ridin' with me."

Soon they were atop his steed, heading toward the wishing well, with Onnleigh perched partly on his lap and partly on the saddle. She found she rather liked being that near to him. With his arms wrapped around her protectively, she felt safe and cared for and wondered if she would ever get used to the feeling. With a certainty, she knew she'd never grow tired of it.

Onnleigh was thankful for the warm cloak Connor had given her as a Yuletide gift. It kept her quite warm against the cold winter air.

Heavy, dark clouds holding the promise of snow made him urge his horse faster along the rolling hills. His men were following in a wide circle per Connor's order.

As they rode, Connor spoke of his childhood, his three brothers, and the one sister they'd lost at an early age. He also told of how hard it had been to lose his parents, then his wife and child.

Onnleigh listened intently, offering nothing about her own upbringing. As far as she was concerned, there was not much to tell. It had been a hard, lonely existence, therefore naught to speak about.

The first snow of winter began to fall before they reached the well, as a strong breeze lifted strands of her hair out of her braid. Onnleigh drew her cloak tighter and dared to lean against Connor for warmth. Happily, he opened his own cloak wide before wrapping it around her. "Next time, I shall remember to bring ye a fur," he promised with a hug.

Soon, they were at the well. Connor dismounted before helping Onnleigh down. With his protective hand at the small of her back, they walked to the well.

"Why be we here?" she asked.

"Do ye ken the legend of the well?"

"Nae, I dunnae ken of a legend," she admitted.

Taking her hand in his, he told her the legend as it had been told to him.

"Long ago, the Vikings came to our lands. Hundreds upon hundreds of years ago. They built this fortress and the walls ye see here," he explained as he glanced about the place.

"Well, one of the Viking soldiers fell in love with a local lass. Seein' how we hated them bein' here, 'twas natural that her parents forbade her to see him. So one night, in desperation, she stole away with the intention of marrying him in secret. Her parents soon learned of their plan, and followed the lovers here. Rather than be separated, they ran to the fort and hid in this well. "

Onnleigh thought it an awfully dangerous place for anyone to hide, but kept her feelings to herself.

"There was a terrible storm that night and the run-off from the mountains that kept the well supplied soon filled it with water until it overflowed, drowning the two lovers."

Her eyes grew wide with surprise. 'Twasn't at all the happy ending she had been expecting.

"Many believe their spirits still wander here. Many also believe that if two lovers tie a lock of their hair together with a weighted ribbon and toss it into the well at Yule time, the spirits will grant them a wish. A wish that will bind them for eternity."

Confused, she stared up at him. "That be a right sad story, Connor," she told him. "I wish to be away from here."

Tilting his head to one side, he asked her why.

"Och! 'Tis bad luck, this place. And I do nae wish to offend any ghosts or spirits!" A sudden gust of wind blew up, whipping bits of dead grass and leaves against the hem of her dress.

Connor drew her to his chest and held her tight. "Do ye ken that I was here a few weeks ago with me grandminny?"

"Aye," she replied as she rubbed her cheek against his chest. "I was here too."

He knew she had been, for Braigh had told him, but he let that matter lie for now. "Do ye ken what I wished for?"

Turning up her face to look at him, she said, "Aye, I do. I could hear ye."

"I be nae a man who believes in ghosts, or fairies, or wishes. At least, I did nae until I met ye."

With a curious expression, she asked him to explain.

"I have been comin' here with me grandminny every year for as long as I can remember. But until this last visit, I never made a wish before. And now look at me."

"Ye wished fer a wife and children and peace," she murmured softly.

"Aye, I did. So do ye understand what that means?"

With a shake of her head, she replied that she did not.

"Ye be a wish and dream come true, lass. Ye be everythin' I wished for that day."

Another shake, this time in disbelief. "Ye be daft," she told him, with the belief that he was just being kind.

"Am I? I think nae. I think there might be somethin' to this auld well. I'd like us to take a lock of our hair and make a wish this night. We shall be married soon and I'd like us to be married a good long time."

Her knotted brow said she questioned his soundness of mind. "And ye think tyin' our hair together and tossin' it into the well will make that happen?"

He gave a slight shrug. "What did ye wish for?"

Admittedly, he had her cornered. She had wished for a warm, safe, and loving home for her daughter. Mayhap there was something to it after all.

Taking his dirk from his belt, he cut a small lock of her hair, then his, before tying them together with a bit of twine. Using a small rock he found lying on the ground, he weighted their entwined hair together.

"Now what shall we wish for?"

She thought long and hard on it. "Many more bairns?" she asked.

That brought a wide smile to his handsome face. "Aye. For many bairns, and continued prosperity for our clan."

"And peace," she added, remembering that had been part of his previous wish.

"And peace," he repeated.

*God willing,* he mused *there will finally be peace for my clan.*

JUST BEFORE THE NEW YEAR, Connor called the MacCallens together for a special meeting. Over Onnleigh's objections, he insisted she be there, right beside him, when he announced to one and all that he was taking her as his wife.

While some of the clanspeople were not behaving with as much hostility as when she had first arrived, she was not so naive as to believe everyone would accept their betrothal.

"Ye dunnae understand the way of it," she was explaining to Connor for what seemed like the hundredth time that day. "Nae all yer people want me here."

Connor, ever the optimist, refused to wait any longer. "And they never will if ye keep yerself hidden away."

Intentionally, she had kept the many blatant instances of rudeness and even hostility towards her a secret. She hadn't even shared those difficult stories with Bridgett or Lorna. Believing 'twas best not to stir the fires, she had kept quiet. That was why Connor fervently believed she was worrying over nothing.

"Have I told ye how beautiful ye look this day?" he asked, smiling fondly at her.

"Only a dozen times," she replied, knowing full well he was trying to change the subject.

"I think Lorna and Bridgett have outdone themselves," he said. She assumed he was referring to the new, dark green woolen gown she wore. "I like yer hair that way."

A warm blush crept up her neck as she touched the intricate braids. Her mouth felt awfully dry, her soft *thank ye* catching in her throat. Onnleigh had quickly learned over the last few weeks that he had a way of disarming her good senses, of making her forget her worries with a few kind, well-placed compliments.

"Are ye ready?"

'Twas Ronald asking that particular question as he stood in the doorway to Onnleigh's new bedchamber. Connor thought it might be best for all concerned if Onnleigh and Nola were moved to a room down the hall. One with a door. The reason was twofold. One, it would help stave off some of the rumors that would surely abound once their announcement was made. And two, 'twould be far more difficult for either of them to give into temptation if they were farther apart.

"Aye," Connor said with a nod. "Are Braigh and Lorna ready?"

"Aye. They be waitin' in the hall, along with Bridgett."

Connor's original idea had been to have the clan assemble out of doors. But a heavy snow had fallen across their lands over the past few days, so the meeting was moved into the gathering room. Though the room was grand and large, it still could not hold every member of the clan, so many spilled out into the hallways. Those that could not fit within were patiently waiting outside the open doors.

"Come," Connor said as he took Onnleigh's hand in his. "Just think," he whispered as they stepped out into the hallway. "In a few weeks, we shall be man and wife, and this will all be over with. Naught more than a distant memory."

Oh, how she wanted with all her heart to believe it would be as easy as Connor was convinced it would be.

CONNOR STEPPED toward the banister and looked down at his people. Onnleigh was just a step behind him, waiting between Braigh and Lorna. Ronald and Bridgett stood to Connor's left. 'Twas as united a front as they could muster, considering the circumstances.

A hush fell over the crowd as all eyes looked up at him. He offered them a warm smile and greeting. "I be glad ye all came to join us this day," he said. "I will nae keep ye long, fer I be certain ye'd all like to return to yer homes, warm fires, and mayhap a dram or two to stave off the cold."

Many in the crowd laughed or chuckled and all agreed with his assessment.

"I have gathered ye all here today to share some verra good news with ye. Some verra good news indeed," he said, his smile undeniable. Turning, he took Onnleigh by the hand and brought her to stand next to him. "Over these past many weeks, I have come to ken Onnleigh *ingen* Grueber as a good woman with a kind and givin' heart. To me family, she has become a good and loyal friend."

Puzzled expressions, whispers of confusion began and swelled amongst the crowd. Connor ignored them and continued.

"But she has become much more than that to me. Onnleigh has won me heart."

Gasps of surprise broke out from below. His people were stunned at the announcement, exchanging bewildered expressions with one another. While some did seem genuinely pleased, there were a small group who looked angry.

Onnleigh fare shook with trepidation. The derisiveness was palpable. Connor gave her hand a gentle squeeze as he ignored those who were less than positive. "We shall be postin' the banns this day. In three weeks time, Onnleigh and I will marry."

As he stared into the eyes of his people, Connor felt, for the very first time, everything Onnleigh had been trying to tell him. While he was relieved to see a good majority of his people appearing happy, 'twas that small handful that made the hair on the back of his neck stand up. However, he fervently believed they would eventually come around to the idea.

"I ken nae all of ye remember Onnleigh, as she has been away from the clan for a good number of years," he said, raising his voice as he looked directly at those clanspeople who seemed less than pleased. "I ken that once ye get to ken her, ye will see her as I and me family do: a kind, generous, warm woman. And I expect each of ye to treat her with respect and kindness."

Those who were in favor of the union cheered and shouted their good wishes. Those who were opposed remained quiet, but they knew Connor's comments were meant solely for them. He was telling them in no uncertain terms how he expected them to treat his betrothed: with nothing less than unmitigated respect.

Giving her hand another gentle squeeze, he kissed Onnleigh rather soundly, leaving no doubt in anyone's mind that he was a man very much in love.

# CHAPTER 10

The following morn, they took their breakfast together in Connor's room, discussing plans on how she could win the clan over. In the end, they decided the best course of action was to be as honest and genuine as possible by simply being herself. Kissing the top of her head, he left her while he went to tend to duties below stairs.

With newfound determination and courage, Onnleigh decided she would set out to prove to Clan MacCallen that she was not the thief or layabout her father had been. If Connor could believe in her, then she should believe in herself.

When it was time for the nooning meal, Onnleigh made herself as clean and as presentable as she could. Wearing the deep indigo gown, she combed her hair until it shone and let it fall down her back. Next, she put Nola in a pretty yellow gown with matching woolens and bonnet, wrapped her in a pretty blue blanket and put her in the sling.

Although she was quite nervous, she did her best not to show it. With her back straight and head held high, she walked down the stairs and into the gathering room. Crossing the floor, she went to the long table where the noonin' meal was spread out. As she picked foods she recognized and some she didn't, she wondered if there would ever come a time where she'd be accustomed to eating so much. Warm bread, dripping with butter and berry jam was quickly becoming her favorite and she was quite happy to see it offered again.

With her trencher full, she took a deep breath and turned to face the crowded room. Dozens of people sat at the tables enjoying their meal and conversations with friends. Who to sit with? She recognized no one.

Taking a chance, she went to the table with the friendliest looking people — a few men and women of varying ages.

"Good day," she said with a smile.

Each looked up at her before exchanging glances with one another. A moment later, they scooted across the benches, just as they had been doing for weeks now. A silent signal that they had no desire for her company.

Her gut tightened as her cheeks burned with humiliation. Refusing to give up or be disheartened, she stepped to the next table, only to be met by the same icy glares and taking up of space so that she could not sit.

Were Connor here with her right now she knew they'd not be treating her with such disrespect. Nay, she had to do this on her own. Pulling her shoulders back she tried the next table.

The results were the same.

Last eve, many of these people had cheered at Connor's announcement. But this morn, they were behaving as if they could not abide the sight of her. What had happened in that short amount of time to change their opinion?

She stood, momentarily lost, in the middle of the room. *What have I e'er done to ye?*

Bridgett wasn't here to protect her. Braigh and Lorna were absent as well. She felt more alone now than she ever had before.

Her attention was drawn away by a loud clicking sound from across the room. Standing there was an auld woman, with silver hair, bright eyes, and a walking stick.

"I be lookin' fer Onnleigh *ingen* Grueber," she said in a loud voice.

All eyes in the room turned to Onnleigh. 'Twas enough to make her knees knock together.

Taking a deep breath and stealing herself for whatever assault the auld woman had in mind for her, she said, "I be her."

The woman eyed her for a long moment before shuffling across the floor. After a long moment of close scrutiny, she smiled and said, "Ye be just as bonny as Connor said."

Onnleigh's shoulders relaxed, but only slightly.

"I be his grandminny, Bruanna," she said. "Come, sup with me so I can get to know ye better."

She turned to face the table that had turned Onnleigh away only moments earlier. They stared at her with confused expressions, unmoving and uncertain.

"Move over, Daniel and Agard, and let us sit," Bruanna said to two middle-aged men.

With a heavy sighs of resignation, the two men parted, allowing plenty of room. Bruanna smiled and let out a groan as she sat and spun around. "I remember a time I could jump on the table and dance 'til the light of morn. Now, 'tis work just to sit at the table."

Onnleigh could not resist smiling as she too took a seat next to Bruanna. Across from them sat another middle-aged man, a young man, mayhap only a few years older than Onnleigh, and a lovely woman with dark hair and brilliant blue eyes.

"Rena, would ye be a dear and get this auld woman some food?" Bruanna asked as she set her walking stick across the table.

"I'll do it," Onnleigh offered sweetly.

With a warm, gnarled hand, Bruanna patted her on the arm. "Nay, ye sit here with me. Rena does nae mind."

Rena quirked a brow, started to respond but thought better of it. "Verra well," she said with more than a bit of frustration.

"I would love a bit of ham," Bruanna said. "With extra gristle. 'Tis good fer me digestion."

Muttering something incoherent, Rena left the table.

"So Seamus the younger," Bruanna directed her full attention to the young man sitting across from her. "Be ye still courtin' Claire *ingen* William?"

The young man's face burned red, but a twinkle lit in his eyes at the mention of the girl's name. "Aye," he said sheepishly.

With a smile and a nod, the auld woman looked pleased. "She be a good one, that lass. Claire *ingen* William will make ye a good wife someday. Does she still make the best jam in Scotia?"

"Aye, she does," he said with a proud smile.

Turning to Onnleigh, she asked, "And ye, lass? Do ye ken how to make jam?"

"Nay," she admitted. "I fear I can ne'er get it to set proper." Her jam usually turned out looking more like a runny sauce than jam.

"Mayhap ye've nae been taught proper." Turning back to the young man, Bruanna said, "I be sure Claire would be quite proud to teach the chief's betrothed how to make a proper jam, aye, Seamus?"

He looked as though he'd just swallowed a slimy bug.

"'Twould be somethin' she could brag about fer years to come, aye? Ye'll ask her, this day?" She didn't wait for his response. "Good! 'Tis settled!"

"What be settled?" Rena asked as she set a trencher in front of Bruanna.

"Yer future daughter-by-law will be teachin' the future wife of the chief how to make jam," Bruanna said with a smile.

The three people all turned to stare at Onnleigh as if she had done something wrong. Before she could point out that Bruanna had suggested it, the auld woman said, "Seamus the aulder here, he be the finest carpenter I've ever kent. Ye should see his fine work!"

The older man stared at Bruanna as if she'd lost her mind.

"Mayhap he could carve a chest fer the chief's bride? Somethin' she could keep her treasures in. 'Twould be an honor, to be certain. Connor would be verra proud to have ye do it."

Slowly, Seamus the aulder set his eating knife down on the table. Looking Bruanna in the eye, he said, "I ken what ye're doin', Bruanna."

"What?" she asked, feigning innocence.

"Ye're appealin' to our pride to get us to do things we'd otherwise nae think to do," he told her pointedly.

The old woman tilted her head ever so slightly. "Ye mean, ye'd nae wish to make a beautiful chest fer the chief's future wife?"

He let out a short breath. "If the chief were inclined to marry someone *else*, then aye, I'd be wishin' to."

Onnleigh's humiliation burned brightly, with cheeks aflame and her eyes downcast.

"Tell me, Seamus the aulder, what is it ye have against me future granddaughter-by-law?"

He seemed surprised that she should ask such a thing. With wide eyes, he stared at the auld woman.

When he did not answer, it prompted his wife to do so on his behalf. "Ye ken who she be, aye?" she asked, leaning over the table slightly.

"Aye, I do," Bruanna replied.

Seamus the younger decided he needed to intercede on Onnleigh's behalf. "Ye all are talkin' as if she be nae here," he said.

Onnleigh chanced a brief glance his way as all eyes at the table turned to her.

"It be nae her fault who she was born to," Bruanna reminded them. "Connor wants her for his wife and that be all that matters."

Seamus the aulder huffed derisively. Rena shook her head as if it were all a great shame. Their son, thankfully, was not of the same mindset.

"Ye were an odd child," he began. "Now I do nae mean that as an insult, mind ye. I think that be why some folks are so taken aback by Connor's announcement. Ye rarely ever spoke and ye were always starin' at people. And ye left and never came back until a few weeks ago and now Connor says he wants to marry ye. Can ye see why people be curious as well as confused?"

Onnleigh played with the fringe on Nola's blanket while she pondered his words. All of that was true. She had been a quiet child and she had stayed away. Perhaps they did not understand the *why* of it all.

"'Twas how I learned," she murmured. Her voice was so soft and low they asked her to repeat herself.

A long moment stretched out before she had the courage to look up. "'Twas how I learned."

They stared back in confusion.

"I did nae have anyone to teach me things after me mum died. So I watched closely what people were doin'. I learned to make soap by watchin' Thomas' mum. I learned to make candles by watchin' Alice's mum."

Rena looked as confused as the rest of them. "But why did ye nae ask us to teach ye these things?"

Onnleigh's chest tightened as a lifetime of memories came crashing through. "I tried, but before I could e'er get a word out, ye all were chasin' me away." Tears brimmed in her eyes, but she refused to shed them lest the others think her weak. "E'er one of ye chased me away, save fer Connor and his mum. Ye all were afraid I'd be stealin' from ye like me da did."

'Twas their turn to feel ashamed. She could see it on their faces, in their eyes. "I stayed away because none wanted me here."

Another long silence filled the air. Finally, Bruanna asked, "Why did ye come back, lass?"

Onnleigh cast a glance her way. "Me da died in the spring. I came to give back the hut and bit of land, fer I was prepared to go seek a life elsewhere. I kent none of ye wanted me here."

Bruanna gave a knowing nod. "Then Connor asked ye to care fer his babe?"

"Aye," she replied softly as she looked down at Nola. "He did. I was sorely tempted to say nay to his offer. But he convinced me this be me clan as much as 'tis anyone else's."

Bruanna patted Onnleigh's hand and smiled at her warmly. "And he be right," she said.

Onnleigh glanced at the others and wondered if they agreed. If they did, they kept their opinions to themselves.

∾

*THE BANNS HAVE BEEN POSTED! Bah!* Helen fumed quietly. Beyond incensed, her hatred toward Onnleigh was building by leaps and bounds. And Connor? Connor would soon rue the day he'd decided to let the bit of filthy trash that was Onnleigh *ingen* Grueber into her home.

Helen had been the chatelaine of this keep ever since William MacCallen had passed away. She'd stepped into the role to help Connor adjust to life as laird and chief. *This is* my *keep, my home!* She fumed as she stepped out into the cold, dreary day.

Doing her best to quash her fury at the two young people, Helen painted on an air of disinterest as she stepped into the kitchens. While she might be furious at this recent turn of events, there was still a keep to run. And it was *her* keep.

Sashaying into the kitchens, she found Louisa at the little table and chair she used as her desk. Louisa looked up from her journal and did something most unusual. She smiled at Helen.

The smile caught her off guard, but only for the briefest of moments. "I would like to speak with ye about the menus fer next week," she said.

Louisa placed the quill into the jar of ink, turned in her chair and said, "There be no need."

Confused, Helen asked, "What do ye mean *there be no need?*"

Not once did Louisa's smile falter. "Just what I said, there be no need. Onnleigh and I went over the menus just this morn."

*Onnleigh?* Just hearing the woman's name sent a burst of fury erupting inside her chest.

Louisa stood then, and looked Helen directly in the eye. She was a few inches shorter than Helen, round and squat, with light hair that had at one time been a deep red. "Aye, Onnleigh. She be the chatelaine now."

"They be nae married," Helen argued.

With a shrug of indifference, Louisa replied, "They will be married and verra soon. Connor thought 'twould be a good idea fer her to start learnin' how to be a proper chatelaine."

Louisa added far too much emphasis to the word *proper* to suit

Helen. Still clinging to her sense of dignity, Helen gave a slow shake of her head. "Connor has nae informed *me* of such a decision. I do nae believe ye be tellin' the truth."

Louisa was so insulted that her nostrils flared and she pursed her lips. But before she could let loose with years of pent up anger, she noticed Connor standing behind Helen.

"She speaks the truth."

STARTLED, Helen spun around at the sound of Connor's voice. He looked nearly as pleased with her distress as Louisa was.

"Why did ye nae come to me to discuss this change?" she finally managed to ask.

"I was plannin' on doin' that verra thing," Connor said. "Mayhap ye would like to discuss this privately?"

Pulling her shoulders back, she affected an air of grace. "Nay," she replied stoically. "We can discuss it now."

"Verra well," Connor began. "As of this moment, ye are nae longer actin' as chatelaine of the keep. Onnleigh will take over all duties, forthwith."

"I would be happy to give Onnleigh my personal instructions on the *proper* way to act as Chatelaine," Helen offered, mustering up a smile that she did not in truth, feel.

"That will nae be necessary," Connor said with a glance toward his cook. "Louisa will be helpin' her in that regard."

There was no way for her to hide her surprise. "The cook?" she asked, stunned and horrified at the same time. The anger built to the point she could no longer contain it. "I suppose ye'll also have the stable master teachin' her how to sew? Or mayhap the smythie to teach her how to serve a proper feast?"

He grinned and gave a nod of his head. "If they have somethin' they'd like to contribute, then aye, I would consider their good advice."

"But nae mine?" Helen's voice was rising in both pitch and loudness. "I have been chatelaine—"

Connor stopped her with a raised hand. "Ye were *actin'* chatelaine. A position I gave ye durin' a time of grief. While I do sincerely appreciate all that ye have done to aid in the runnin' of the keep, I must now give that position to me betrothed."

*His betrothed? Bah!* Helen wanted to scream, to scratch out his eyes for being so unkind toward her. After all she had done for him these past years? "I suppose ye'll be wantin' me to leave the keep as well?"

"Aye, I would. I think 'twould be best fer all concerned if ye were to return to yer cottage. Ye and Margaret. While I ken ye mean only to help, I think 'twould be best if Onnleigh could learn her new position without interference."

Connor's grin was as off-putting as Louisa's. The fact that they were enjoying her distress did not go unnoticed. Neither would it go unchallenged.

'TWAS DIFFICULT TO REMAIN CALM. But calm she must. With heads held high, Helen and Margaret quietly moved their things out of the keep. While most would have been grateful to have a home to return to, Helen found no comfort in it. She and Margaret spent the better part of the day cleaning the large space and putting things in order. As soon as it was presentable, Helen invited two of her closest companions over to help her wallow in her self-pity.

"They are to be married the last day of January," she said as she offered warm cider to the three women sitting at her table. Two of the women were her oldest friends - Eleana and Trudee - the third, her daughter Margaret.

Where Eleana was short and round, with pewter colored hair and dark blue eyes, Trudee was taller, leaner, and had somehow managed to maintain her golden tresses. As far as Helen was concerned, each were as intelligent as a box of rocks. But what they may have lacked in intelligence, they made up for in loyalty.

Of course, it helped knowing their secrets. Secrets that would ruin not only their reputations but the carefully crafted lives they had somehow managed to carve out for themselves. Helen knew those dark secrets and betimes used them to keep the two women in line.

Her friends were no happier about Connor's announcement than she. Of course, had Helen been happy about the announcement, the two women would have been as well. Malleable minds made for better friends.

"What do ye intend to do?" Eleana asked as she sipped the warm cider.

Helen pretended to think long and hard on the question. Of course, she had been up most of the night, trying to craft a plan that would bring any wedding plans to an abrupt halt. The problem was, she didn't have a secret to hold over Onnleigh's head. Oh, she knew the girl possessed one, but Helen was having the damnedest time trying to figure out what it was.

Everyone had secrets. *Everyone.* If only...If only she could gain knowledge of Onnleigh's, then she could use it to force the girl to leave. Come hell or high water, Connor would marry Margaret.

"She's bewitched him," Trudee said. "'Tis the only thing that makes a lick of sense to me."

"Bah!" Eleana exclaimed dismissively. "She has turned his head is all, with that red hair of hers. 'Tis nae a bewitchment, 'tis lust."

Trudee shrugged her shoulder as if she did not care what her friend's opinion was. "Call it what ye will, the result is the same. Connor wishes to marry her. Bewitched or lustin', he still wants to marry her."

Helen hadn't been listening closely, for she was too lost in trying to figure out what secrets the trash Onnleigh might have. The word 'bewitched' brought her back to the moment. *Bewitched.*

In the past, if she couldn't garner a person's secret, she would sometimes spread a rumor based on nothing more than a simple lie. The simple lie would build and grow until 'twas believed to be God's truth.

'Twas then the idea formed. She could see it as clearly as the three women sitting at her table. Joy bubbled up from her stomach. 'Twas all she could do not to jump on top of the table and dance a jig! But a calm head was called for at this juncture. A very calm head.

"Ye ken, I was once walkin' near the hovel Onnleigh shared with her da…"

Telling the lie was as easy as breathing. And oh, what a lie it was. There was not an ounce of truth to it. There didn't need to be.

Helen knew the moment she finished telling her tale Eleana and Trudee wouldn't be able to get out of her home fast enough to share the information. And that was what she needed, for the tale to be told again and again until it was believed to be nothing but the truth.

Before the end of the week, the *rumor* that Onnleigh *ingen* Grueber was practicing witchcraft would be spread wide enough to stop the wedding.

ONNLEIGH DID NOT WANT to leave the comfort of her warm bed. But the fire in her brazier had died at some point during the night, leaving the air in her room frigid. When she leaned over to check on her daughter, she could see her own breath. Nola slept peacefully in her cradle, but her little nose and cheeks were red from the cold.

The only light illuminating the room came from a small crack in the fur that covered her window.

Wrapping a fur around her shoulders, Onnleigh set about restarting the brazier. Rubbing her hands together to take out the sting from the cold, she glanced up at the window. Snow had drifted in through the crack, leaving behind a little pile of the fluffy white powder. Quickly, she went to the window and peeked out. As far as the eye could see, the lands were covered, glistening in the pre-dawn morn colors of purple and indigo. Sparkling brightly as if some ancient giant had tossed diamonds hither and yon from the low hanging moon. 'Twould not be long before the sun rose.

Shivering, she tightened the fur as best she could before returning to her bed. The sheets were chilly, causing her to shiver again. Pulling the furs over her ears, she waited for the room to warm again and for sleep to return.

Her thoughts were of Connor, as they so often were. In a few short weeks, she would be his wife. Worry settled in. She didn't know how to be a wife to anyone, let alone a clan chief. She fretted quietly that she would somehow muck it up. The last thing she wanted to do was to be an embarrassment to him.

When she finally drifted off to sleep, she dreamt of Connor and their future together. Always smiling at her, he seemed quite proud to call her wife. In that dream, she was dressed in a beautiful green gown, her hair fashioned prettily, with little flowers and dark green ribbons woven through it. She had the sense of being at peace, feeling nothing but love and adoration from Connor and the many children she had apparently given life to. Children of all ages surrounded her, smiling up at her adoringly, proudly.

They were bathed in the warmth of bright sunshine, surrounded by spring grass and newly blossomed flowers. 'Twas the most peaceful she had ever felt, even if 'twas just a dream.

Suddenly, she heard, or rather felt, a low rumble of thunder. Soon, the sky was as black as pitch, darker than night, and the thunder grew louder and louder. Her children sought refuge behind her.

Connor's bright smile faded rapidly. A most dark expression came upon him. She had done something wrong, something horrible. Something unforgivable. But what that something was, she didn't know. She could only feel his disgust toward her.

Their children went to him at once, all bearing the same expression of loathing as their father. Moments later, they were all walking away, hanging their heads in shame. She called out to them, crying, begging and pleading for forgiveness. Her pleas went unanswered, for they could not hear her over the roar of the thunder. Soon, they disappeared into the darkness, leaving her all alone. Not even Nola was at her side.

Cold enveloped her, seeping into her bones. Her tears turned to ice, dropping to the cold earth and crashing, breaking into countless pieces.

She was all alone in this world once again. Completely, devastatingly *alone*.

～

ONNLEIGH WOKE, her cheeks damp from crying, her chest heavy with a sorrow she didn't think she'd felt since losing her mother. Afraid, nay terrified, she scurried from her bed, grabbed Nola, and headed to Connor's room.

Using the light of the fire to guide her way, she quickly went to his side. He slept on his back, one arm resting over his eyes. His room was warm, much warmer than her own. For the longest of moments, she simply stood, staring down at him as quiet tears fell.

He must have sensed her presence, for he woke and sat up as he grabbed a large dirk from under his pillow. "Onnleigh?" he said, his voice scratchy with sleep. "What be the matter?"

The concern in his eyes, the soft, warm timber of his voice nearly sent her to her knees. *Be strong,* she chastised herself. Taking in a deep breath, choking on a sob, she said, "I cannae marry ye."

Shaking his head in disbelief, he let out a sigh, replaced the dirk and smiled. "Come now," he said, sitting up on the edge of the bed. "Tell me why ye have changed yer mind."

The cold from the floor began to seep into her woolens. With a shiver, she said, "It matters no' if I be a good wife to ye and give ye many children," she said with a sniffle. "Some day ye will see the folly of yer choice and leave me."

At seeing her shiver, he wrapped his arms around her and pulled her to sit next to him. He grabbed the fur and wrapped it around her shoulders. "That will never happen," he told her.

"But 'twill!" she argued tearily.

"What has brought this about?" he asked, holding her close.

"I, I had a dream," she admitted as she wiped the tears from her cheeks.

Connor chuckled warmly. "A dream?"

She nodded. "'Twas a nightmare, Connor. We had many children and seemed verra happy. But I did somethin' to anger ye and ye left me. Ye took all our children away. Even Nola."

With a gentle hand, he touched her cheek and turned her to look at him. "Lass, I swear to ye, I will *never* take Nola or any of our future children away from ye. I will never leave ye."

She could only pray he would keep that promise.

# CHAPTER 11

On a dark, gloomy day, ten days before Connor and Onnleigh were to marry, a messenger from the Randall clan appeared at their borders. The young man was brought immediately to Connor.

The rather nervous young lad now stood, albeit a bit shakily, in the gathering room of the MacCallen keep. The snow that crusted his fur cloak and boots began to melt, leaving puddles of water on the stone floor.

He was surrounded by a wall of some two-dozen MacCallen warriors. Connor was quite proud of his men, for each and every one assembled here were the best trained and most ruthless of his clan. Their presence was meant to intimidate and it was working quite well. The poor lad looked ready to shite himself.

Connor reckoned the lad could not be more than eight and ten years. As skinny as a sapling tree, with blond hair and intense blue eyes, the boy was doing his best to not look too afraid. But who would not be afraid, surrounded by the likes of the MacCallen warriors?

"What are ye called?" Connor asked.

The boy swallowed hard. "Elgin," he said. "Elgin Randall."

"Well, Elgin Randall, what message does yer laird send ye with?" Connor finally asked, looking directly at the lad.

Without thinking, the young man reached for something inside his cloak. Immediately, every sword in the room was drawn and pointed directly at him. He paused, swallowed hard again, his eyes as wide as trenchers. "'Tis naught but my laird's missive."

Silence stilled the air, not one man ready to sheath his sword on the word of a Randall.

"Slowly," Conner warned him with a nod.

Carefully, he pulled his cloak open, the scroll clearly visible, tucked into his sword belt. Connor took the offered missive and stood by the roaring fire to read it. Moments ticked by as the warriors waited with an eerie calmness. Elgin shifted his weight from one foot to the other, undoubtedly wishing he was anywhere but here.

When Connor finished reading the missive a second time, he rolled the parchment and clenched it in his hand. "Tell yer laird I agree to his terms."

CONNOR'S WARRIORS waited until Elgin was escorted from the keep before plying their laird with questions. Connor raised a hand for quiet. "The Randall, it seems, wants to meet with me."

Curious glances were shared amongst his men, but they remained quiet. Ronald and Braigh stepped forward, standing on either side of their brother. 'Twas a show of support for Connor.

"And ye agreed?" one of the older warriors finally put to voice what everyone else was thinking.

"Aye, I have agreed to the meetin'."

More uncertain looks and glances between his men. Connor pulled his shoulders back and let out a slow breath. "'Tis a meetin' to discuss peace betwixt our clans," Connor told them. "But I shall nae agree to anythin' until I have discussed it with all of ye. I will take yer opinions into consideration."

Someone at the back of the room scoffed. 'Twas Darrin MacCallen, the nephew of their stable master. A young man of two and twenty who had excelled in training—one Connor believed had a good head on his shoulders. "Darrin?" Connor said, stepping toward him.

Concern and a bit of embarrassment were visible in the young man's eyes.

"Ye have an issue?"

Darrin glanced at those around him as if he were looking for support. None would offer it until they heard what he had to say.

"Do ye nae believe I will listen to my most trusted men?" Connor asked.

Darrin was growing tense under Connor's scrutinization, his eyes darting from one person to the next. A light sheen of perspiration broke out on his forehead. He cleared his throat before answering. "Ye did nae ask our opinion when ye chose Onnleigh," he finally blurted out.

A hush fell over the room as Connor stared the young man down. He had wondered who, if any, amongst his men, might disagree with his choice of bride. "Ye do nae agree with my decision?" Connor asked, raising one brow. "Ye object to Onnleigh?"

"That is nae what I said or meant," Darrin replied.

"Then, pray tell, enlighten me," Connor told him.

He stammered to get the words out. "I meant only that 'twas a verra important decision. One ye did nae come to us with. Who ye marry does affect the entire clan."

"How will my marriage to Onnleigh *affect* the clan?" Connor asked. "She be one of us. She be a MacCallen. Was there someone else ye thought I should marry?"

Darrin shook his head slowly. "Nae, no one else," he replied sheepishly.

"Have ye objections to Onnleigh?" Connor asked, his voice calm, his tone even.

Darrin's silence said more than words could have. Connor turned to face every man in the room. "Do any of ye have objections? If ye do, I would hear them now."

Fergus MacCallen stepped forward. He was one of the older warriors, in his forties, with long dark hair and piercing blue eyes.

"There has been talk, m'laird. Some believe ye could have chosen better."

"Better?" Connor asked with a raised brow.

Fergus nodded once. "Aye, better. Ye do remember who her father was, aye?"

"Of course I remember," Connor replied. "But Onnleigh, I can assure ye, be nothin' like the man who sired her."

Fergus smiled wryly. "On that, I would have to agree."

Confused, Connor's brow drew into a hard line.

"I am only tellin' ye what some of our clanspeople be sayin'. I, however, do nae agree with them."

Connor smiled ever so slightly and nodded, a signal for Fergus to continue.

"If she had been anythin' like her da, we would have heard of it," Fergus said, looking directly at Darrin. "But never once, in all these many years, has anyone even uttered the lass's name. 'Twas her da who did the stealin'. 'Twas he who was a drunkard and layabout. But can any of ye here say the same of his daughter?"

Several shook their heads.

"I think the only thing Onnleigh ever stole was our laird's heart," Fergus said with a wry grin. "And I do believe that was a stealin' our laird does nae object to, if the smile on his face be any indication."

Most of the men chuckled and smiled.

"If anyone in this clan objects to our laird's decision, 'tis only because they are weak-minded fools who would rather believe rumors than truth," someone added over the din.

"But can she be trusted?"

Connor could not see who asked that particular question.

Braigh stepped forward and looked out at the crowd. "Do ye truly believe Connor be stupid enough to fall for a lass who could nae be trusted?"

More murmurs from the men as they openly discussed the matter. Connor felt it would be better to listen, at least for a short while. The men needed to have this discussion here, now, and in the open. Better that than to let those who objected stew and become frustrated or angry.

In the end, those who might have been uncertain about Connor's upcoming marriage decided to accept it.

~

ONNLEIGH TRIED to look happy when Connor told her about the Randall. They sat in her chamber in front of the roaring fire. Nola was on Connor's lap chewing on his fingers whilst he gave Onnleigh the good news.

"This could be the beginning of peace," Connor told her. His eyes were filled with so much hope.

Onnleigh knew that above all else, he wanted peace for their clan. It was the one thing he'd been working toward for a good long while. "Can it nae wait until after we are wed?" she asked, her heart cracking with the mere thought of him leaving her here alone before they were good and properly wed.

"I have given that some thought," he told her. "But I fear that if we do nae meet now, the Randall's could align themselves with the McCrearys."

Even Onnleigh was smart enough to know that would not bode well for Connor or his people. Reluctantly, she acquiesced. "I ken how important it be to ye," she said. "I truly hope ye finally get the peace ye have desired for so long."

He smiled warmly as he gently bounced Nola on his knee. "Aye, I have desired peace for too many years to count. But ye, Onnleigh, are more important to me than anything else in this world."

There was no doubt in her mind that he meant what he said. 'Twas difficult for her not to fling herself into his arms. If he hadn't been holding Nola, she would have done just that.

There was a twinkle in his eyes that bespoke a promise. A promise that he would always keep her safe, no matter the cost. In all her years, she had dreamed of having someone special who would look at her with adoration instead of disdain. Tears threatened, her skin tingling and warm.

"I fear I be missin' ye already," she admitted.

"Ye do?" he asked playfully with a glint of pride in his bright eyes.

"Of course I do," she told him as she fought hard not to cry. She would wait to shed her tears after he left. "Connor, promise me ye will come back to me."

With an affectionate smile, he stood and kissed her most passionately, stealing her breath away. Oh, how his kisses made her feel! Alive, excited, and eager for more. "I love ye, Connor MacCallen," she whispered after he broke the kiss.

"And I love ye, Onnleigh," he replied, with a rather pleased grin. He knew how his kisses affected her and took great pride in it. "And I promise I will return to ye."

Onnleigh understood how important this meeting was. Not only for Connor, but for the entire clan. Weeks ago, she had even suggested Connor reach out to the Randalls to gain an alliance. This could be the pathway to the peace Connor had always sought.

Understanding the importance, however, did not make her feel any better about being left behind. "Are ye certain we cannae go with ye?" she asked once again.

"Nay, lass," he replied. "'Twill be far too dangerous."

*More dangerous than bein' here alone?* she wondered nervously.

"Ye will be safe here, Onnleigh. I will be leaving most of our men behind to guard ye and the keep."

'Twas probably foolish to fret over it, but she could not help herself. Soon, she would be his wife. There would undoubtedly be times in the future when he would have to leave her behind. *Ye might as well get used to it now,* she told herself. 'Twas the thought of being completely alone that worried her most. He'd not be here to protect her.

Sensing her worry, he placed Nola in her cradle before pulling Onnleigh onto his lap. Holding her close, he did his best to soothe her worries. "Braigh and Lorna will be here, as well as Bridgett, to keep ye company. I will only be gone for three days."

Lest he think her weak, she decided then and there to convey an air of strength and calm. She'd not send him off worrying about her. "Ye'd best return to me, Connor MacCallen," she sighed against his neck.

"I promise, lass," he said as he kissed her forehead. "I promise."

JUST HOURS before they were to leave for the Randall keep, Braigh and Lorna received most devastating news. Lorna's last living relative, her older sister Myrna, had given birth. She was not due until the end of February. The babe had been stillborn and Myrna was not expected to live through the end of the day.

With a heavy heart, Braigh went at once to his brother to explain the situation to him. Connor was in the gathering room, giving last minute orders to those men he would leave behind to guard the keep.

Connor took one look at his crestfallen brother and knew at once that something was seriously wrong. Braigh explained to him about the missive he'd just received.

"Ye need to take yer wife to say goodbye to her sister," Connor told him.

"But what of the Randall?" Braigh asked, still genuinely concerned that the Randall meeting was naught more than a trap.

"I will take Ronald with me," Connor said as looked at the map he had spread out on the table. "I want ye to take at least ten men with ye to the Mackintosh keep."

"Nay," Braigh replied. "I do nae want to jeopardize the safety of the keep whilst we are both away."

Connor would brook no argument. "I will nae argue it with ye. If ye wish to take yer wife to say her goodbyes to her sister, then ye will take ten men with ye. I will reduce the number goin' with me to thirty. The rest can stay behind and guard Onnleigh, Nola, and our home."

"And what if I am right?" Braigh asked, his brow drawn into a deep line of concern and worry. "Then ye will be the last MacCallen standin' and 'twill be up to ye to avenge our deaths."

Whilst said in jest, Braigh found no humor in it.

THE RANDALL KEEP was a day's ride from the MacCallens. A good eight hours in fair weather. Lord only knew how long it would take them now, for the snow was as deep as a horse's knees. Thick, cold, and crusty. The only thing to be glad for was the fact the wind had died down and the sun was shining brightly.

Onnleigh stood on the steps of the keep, looking beautiful, if not despondent, in her regal emerald green gown. 'Twas another addition to her growing wardrobe—yet one more gift from Connor.

Bridgett was above stairs, watching over Nola, whilst Onnleigh bid him goodbye.

"I shall return in three days time," Connor reminded her. His smile was warm, lighting his eyes. He was doing his best to reassure her that she need not worry.

"Ye promise?" she asked as she rested her head against his chest.

"I do so promise, lass." He hugged her gently, patting her back as he told her once again how much he loved her. "Ye mean more to me than ye could ever imagine, Onnleigh."

She'd rather be gutted than to cry in front of him now, or in front of the other clanspeople. Putting on a most brave front, she pulled away. "Ye best come back to me, Connor MacCallen. We have a weddin' to attend in less than a week."

"I would nae miss it for the world," he told her.

# CHAPTER 12

*A* well-laid plan was useless if it was not executed with precision.

And that was what Helen needed this day: her cohorts and companions to execute each of their roles without any mistakes. She couldn't afford even the tiniest of errors.

Since the day Connor had made his eloquent speech and announcement, she had done nothing but think on the best way to get Onnleigh out of the chief's life, and for good. For days, she had tried to find something with which to blackmail Onnleigh into leaving of her own accord. But try as she might, she could find nothing. Not even the tiniest crumb of information could be found on the young woman. Staying away from the clan and keep for all those years worked to Onnleigh's advantage, not Helen's.

The rumors about witchcraft would have worked had Connor not interfered and stopped them before they could take their full affect. The bloody fool.

Helen was growing desperate, fully prepared to sneak into the keep and slice Onnleigh's throat whilst she slept. But as the fates would have it —she refused to call it luck or fortune because she believed in neither — word came that Connor was leaving for three days to meet with the Randalls.

And so it began, the first steps of her plan fell into place nicely. Just a few milk cows here and there, that had mysteriously stopped giving milk. She owed that bit of ingenuity to her knowledge of herbs.

Next, a few chickens disappearing, only to be found scattered with their heads missing. Small, little details like those made for the best of plans.

And just an hour before Connor left, a goat was found hanging from a tree just outside the walls of the keep. Its heart was missing, but naught else. Just one dead goat hanging from a tree. She owed that deed to her daughter, Margaret. Aye, even Margaret had secrets. Deep, dark secrets that may or may not have had some truth to them.

Connor wasn't even aware of the goat's death when he left, which also played to her favor.

'Twasn't fate that intervened next by calling Braigh away. Nay, Helen arranged all that herself. By the time anyone realized 'twas naught more than tactic to get Braigh away from the keep, well, Onnleigh and the bastard child would be dead.

THE NEXT STEP in Helen's devious plan to do away with Onnleigh *ingen* Grueber and the bastard child Connor was so fond of was, by far, the most important.

It would involve duplicity of the highest sort. Timing was everything at this juncture.

Of course, the clan was in an uproar by noon the following day, thanks to her good work and the fast-moving lips of Eleana and Trudee. *Did ye hear? Margery's milk cow quit givin' milk! And so did auld Fergus and Annie's! Did ye also hear about the chickens? And just this morn, the goat? Heads cut off all the chickens, ye ken. And the goat was missin' it's heart! I tell ye, it be witchcraft, pure and simple.*

Rumors flew as fast as an eagle, enraging one person after another, until nearly the entire clan was in a frenzied state. Just as Helen had known they would be.

*"Nothin' like this ever happened until Onnleigh came back,"* Helen had whispered into Deidre MacKelvey's ear.

*"I wonder what she was doin' out in the woods fer all those years?"* Helen had asked Mona MacCallen. To which Mona replied, *"I heard she was practicin' her spells! Did ye ken Margery's cow quit given milk? There be no other explanation fer a good milk cow to suddenly stop given milk!"*

Before she knew it, the rumors she had begun earlier were getting back to her. Enid MacCallum stopped by Helen's croft that evening. The poor woman was fit to be tied with dread and worry. *"Did ye hear about the goat?"* she asked breathlessly as she fidgeted with the hem of her shawl. "Dead, it was! Hangin' from a tree with its heart and entrails missin'!"

"Aye, I had heard," Helen replied. "Who would do such a thing?"

"'Twas Grueber's daughter, Onnleigh, I just ken it!" Enid said, looking worried and angry at the same time.

"What makes ye say such?" Helen asked, feigning ignorance whilst trying to hide her glee.

"Och!" Enid cried. "Did ye nae hear? All those years of livin' away from us, out in those woods? She was practicin' her dark arts, she was."

"Nay!" Helen murmured, looking just as appalled as poor Enid.

Enid leaned in and lowered her voice. "I heard that when Grueber died, she cut out his heart and offered it as a sacrifice to the devil!"

Helen hadn't started *that* particular rumor. Still, she was glad they were taking flight and turning more terrifying and gruesome. 'Twould all work to her advantage.

"What are we to do?" Enid cried.

"I do nae ken," Helen replied.

Enid swiped away a tear from her cheek. "She will cast spells on all our menfolk, Helen! Soon, all our cows will be dry, our chickens will quit layin', and our goats will be dead!" She actually began to tremble with worry. "And what of our children, Helen? How will we protect them? Ye must do somethin' about this, Helen!"

And those were the words she had been waiting to hear.

WHILST HAVING the clan lathered into a frenzy and gaining a taste for blood was important, it was not *the* most important part of her plan. What she needed most was a way to get the warriors Connor had left behind to leave. And what better way to do that than to tell them Connor and his party had been attacked some ten miles from the keep?

She owed that bit of duplicity and wonderful acting to Darwud MacAllen. Months ago, Helen had caught him in the throes of passion with a woman who was not his wife. She'd been sitting on that bit of information for a long, long while. Darwud knew that should his wife find out about his infidelity again, she would leave him. So keep it to herself she did, to be used when 'twas most needed. And today, 'twas needed.

'Twas just after the sun began to set that she put the next part of her plan into place. Just as she had planned, Darwud came running up to the gates of the keep, looking as though he'd been chased by a rabid bear. He had dozens upon dozens of people running after him.

"Call the alarm!" he yelled to the guards. "Call the alarm!"

The guards began to scurry to find out why Darwud and the others were running toward the keep.

"Connor has been attacked! The Randalls and McCearys be headin' this way!" he shouted, out of breath, falling down in the deep snow. "Call the alarm!"

The guards needn't be asked twice.

ONNLEIGH WAS in her room with Bridgett when they heard the commotion taking place outside.

"What on earth is goin' on?" Bridgett asked. Onnleigh had no earthly idea. With a shrug of her shoulders, she scooped Nola up and they rushed out of the chamber and into the hallway. They were about to descend the stairs when the doors to the gathering room burst open.

Fear and dread enveloped Onnleigh when she saw Darwud, with his sword drawn, blood dripping from the tip. Right behind him were Helen and Margaret.

Darwud's eyes were filled with a murderous rage, his chest heaving up and down. When he caught sight of her, he scowled, drawing one hand into a fist.

Onnleigh gasped, trying to take tentative steps backward. She knew that look, had seen it that day more than a year ago, when he'd struck her not once, but twice. Try as she might, she could not will her feet to move.

Helen noticed her too. The smile she gave her was enough to make Onnleigh's stomach drop to her toes.

"Good lord," Bridgett murmured as she took Onnleigh's arm. "Run!"

~

THEY COULDN'T MOVE FAST ENOUGH. Bridgett pushed Onnleigh through the door to the chamber. She was trying to bar the door when Darwud shoved it open with one shoulder.

Bridgett cursed as she fell to the floor.

Holding her daughter tightly, Onnleigh scurried to the far wall, pressing herself against it. Her fingers trembled, her legs feeling as strong as water.

Darwud panted as he stood over Bridgett. Helen and Margaret swept themselves inside, stepping over her without so much as a glance her way.

Onnleigh could not find her voice. She wanted to scream, to cry out, but the sound was lodged firmly in her throat.

Helen stood directly in front of her, still smiling that wicked, ugly smile. "Margaret warned ye, yet ye refused," she hissed.

"She has every right to be here, ye auld hag!" Bridgett screamed.

Darwud kicked her in the side with a heavy boot.

Hugging her side, Bridgett glowered up at him. "Ye will regret doin' that."

His booted foot landed harder this time, sending Bridgett rolling to her side.

Anger filled Onnleigh's heart, allowing her the strength, finally, to speak. "What are ye doin' here?" she asked Helen.

"I be settin' things to rights," Helen said. "Connor *will* be marryin' Margaret, nae ye."

Onnleigh scoffed openly. "He will ne'er marry her."

Helen quirked one brow. "Think ye nae?" she asked. "He will once the clan sees he was bewitched by ye. They will demand it, and Connor will be so grief-stricken and so worried about losin' the clan, that he will do anythin' to keep it together."

Onnleigh's brow drew into a hard line. "Grief-stricken?" She regretted asking the question the moment the words passed over her lips.

Helen's smile grew more devious, more malicious. "Aye," she said with a nod. "Devastated at losin' ye and that bastard child."

Onnleigh's eyes grew wide, horrified, as understanding settled in. Helen meant not only to kill her, but her babe as well. Bile rose in the back of her throat. Refusing to show Helen how terrified she truly was, Onnleigh lifted her chin defiantly. "Ye will burn in hell fer this."

Helen lashed out, her hand burning across Onnleigh's cheek. It stung, but Onnleigh refused to shed one tear in front of this woman. Helen grabbed a handful of Onnleigh's hair, forcing her to look at her.

"I do nae believe in hell," she seethed. "But ye soon will."

AT HELEN'S ORDER, Darwud pulled Bridgett to her feet, the tip of his sword aimed right at her throat. Bridgett remained silent, but if looks could kill, Darwud would have been dead.

"Take the babe," Helen ordered Margaret.

Margaret did not move. Onnleigh could see Margaret was battling with something. Perhaps, just perhaps, she was not as keen on the idea of murder as her mother was.

"Please," Onnleigh pleaded. "She be an innocent babe. Please, do nae hurt her."

Margaret's eyes darted between Onnleigh and her mother. "The babe be an innocent," Margaret whispered.

Without taking her eyes from Onnleigh, Helen spoke to her daughter. "If ye do nae do this, by morn, everyone in the clan will ken."

Onnleigh didn't know what Helen meant, but whatever it was, it shook away any doubts Margaret might have been harboring. She stepped forward and began to pull Nola from Onnleigh's arms.

"Nay!" Onnleigh cried. "She be an innocent babe!" Her heart thundered against her breast, her palms damp. Sweat began to trickle down the back of her neck as she pleaded for mercy for her daughter. "She is just a bairn," Onnleigh sobbed, refusing to let go. "She has ne'er hurt anyone."

"Give Margaret that child," Helen ordered. "Or ye will both die now."

Tears streamed down Onnleigh's cheeks. *How could anyone be this cruel? I cannae just give her my babe!*

Margaret shoved her hand between Onnleigh and the bundle in her arms. As she did, she leaned in and whispered in her ear. "Do as she says and all will be well."

Furiously, Helen demanded to know what Margaret had said.

"I simply told her I will kill this babe in front of her so she might watch her die."

Satisfied, Helen nodded. "Take the babe to the fairy tree," she told Margaret.

Fear seized Onnleigh's heart. "Nay!" The fairy tree was more than two miles from the keep. 'Twas a place mother's sometimes left babes when they were ill. It was done with the belief that if the babe was still there by morn, it would be healed. If the babe was gone, then 'twas believed the fairies had taken it to be raised as one of their own. More often than not, the babes would be found dead, dying either from their illness or exposure to the elements.

It was the dead of winter. Nola would not be able to survive more than an hour. Onnleigh screamed as Margaret pulled the babe from her arms. "Nay! Do nae do this!"

Margaret hurried away, slipping past Bridgett. Darwud glanced down at the bundle in Margaret's arms. A brief glimpse of the crying babe was all it took for his smug expression to evaporate in an instant. Bewilderment turned to rage as he spun to look at Onnleigh.

In that brief moment, she realized he knew. He knew 'twas his babe Margaret was carrying to its death. For the briefest of moments, Onnleigh hoped and prayed he would do something to stop her. Instead, he pursed his lips and glowered at her.

Her heart cracked, shattering into inestimable pieces. He knew the babe was his, yet he was not going to intervene. Darwud would rather let the child die than to admit he was her father.

Onnleigh could not breathe, could not find the strength to move. *Nola! Nola!* Silently she screamed, for she did not have the strength or wind to speak. Falling to her knees, she begged Helen to show mercy on the babe.

"I will do anythin' ye ask, anythin'. I will go far away and ne'er come back. Just please, do nae hurt her!"

Helen stepped away, the contempt she felt towards Onnleigh etched into the lines of her face. Shaking her head, she looked at Bridgett then back at Onnleigh.

"On the morrow, ye both shall be tried as witches. Then ye shall burn."

PEOPLE HAD GATHERED in the courtyard. How many, they could not tell, but it sounded to Onnleigh and Bridgett like a thousand angry voices. The air vibrated with hatred and the call for Onnleigh's death. She could hear them chanting *"Burn the witch! Burn the witch!"*

When Bridgett had asked Darwud where he was taking them, he

replied with a sharp slap to her cheek. Onnleigh tried to intervene, to help her friend back to her feet. Enraged, Darwud turned his wrath on Onnleigh before dragging the two women at sword point to the dungeon. Blood trickled from her nose and broken lip.

They were now locked away in the deepest, darkest part of the dungeon. One lit torch at the opposite end of the space offered the only light. Bridgett insisted the space hadn't been used in decades. But to Onnleigh, it still smelled of death and despair.

Feeling hopeless, they huddled together in the corner of the cell. Terrified and angry, they clung to each other for warmth as well as support. Cold seeped up through the damp, cold stone floor, chilling both of them. 'Twas a long while before either spoke.

"I hate that woman," Bridgett said with a shudder. "I hate her and her daughter."

Onnleigh didn't have the energy to reply. Weeping, she clung to Bridgett, unable to control her anguish. At this very moment, Margaret was on her way to put her babe in the fairy tree. Nola would undoubtedly be dead before the evening meal.

She wept openly and without restraint. Her heart, she was certain, had quit beating. Nothing, nothing could ever take away this pain and sorrow. Silently, she prayed for her own death. There was no reason to go on anymore. Let them do to her whatever they would, for she no longer cared.

"Wheest," Bridgett whispered as she tried to offer some form of comfort. There was no point in it. "Ronald and Connor will save us," Bridgett said. "Just ye wait and see."

"I do nae care about meself," Onnleigh cried. "'Tis Nola I cry fer!"

"I ken, Onnleigh. I ken. " Bridgett said as she smoothed Onnleigh's hair. "But I refuse to give up hope. If I do, I will nae survive to the morn."

"Hope?" Onnleigh scoffed at the idea. "I lost all hope when Margaret took Nola from me. I just want to die!"

Bridgett grabbed her by the shoulders. "Do nae say that!" she scolded her. "Do nae say that! Ronald will come fer us, ye will see. He will!"

"But what about Nola?" Onnleigh wept against her friend's chest. "What about Nola?"

Bridgett swallowed the tears that threatened. "God will watch out fer her, I ken he will."

Onnleigh sniffled and pulled away to look into Bridgett's eyes. Deep down she knew there was no hope for them, not for any of them. But Bridgett was so utterly hopeful, even though tears clung to her lashes. Aye, Onnleigh was quite certain they were going to die on the morrow. She would do whatever she could to make Bridgett's last hours on earth a bit more peaceful. If that meant falsely hoping that somehow Connor would come to rescue them, then she would.

"Do ye truly think they will come fer us?" she asked, swiping away tears on the sleeve of her dress.

"Aye, I do," Bridget replied. She did sound rather hopeful. Mayhap Onnleigh should cling to hope as well.

Silently, she turned her thoughts heavenward.

*Please, God, watch over my babe. Please.*

"BRIDGETT, BE THAT YE?" a low, deep voice whispered from across the way.

Both women sat upright, their eyes scanning the dark. "Who goes there?" Bridgett asked.

A slight groan filtered in before the man answered. "'Tis me, Fergus," he replied. "Be Onnleigh with ye?"

"Aye," Bridgett replied as they scurried to the bars. "Please, Fergus, let us out of here!"

"I fear I cannae do that, Bridgett. I be locked in here with ye. I think me arm be broken."

Their hope at rescue fell away in the flutter of a heartbeat.

"Darrin be with me," Fergus groaned. "I fear he be worse off than I."

Bridgett and Onnleigh clung to the bars of their cell, craning their necks, trying to see the men.

"I be here as well." That voice came from the opposite direction. "'Tis me, Red John." Onnleigh could not remember meeting him before. However, she took a good measure of comfort in knowing she and Bridgett were not completely alone.

"Are ye well?" Onnleigh asked, her hope rising once again.

"Other than me poundin' skull, aye, I be well," Red John called out to them.

"I cannae wait to get me hands on Darwud," came yet another voice from farther down. "I plan on reachin' into his chest and pullin' his heart out."

"Be that ye, Clarence?" Red John asked.

"Aye, it be me," he replied, his deep, scratchy voice echoing off the walls. "The bloody fool damn near gutted me!"

"Watch yer language in front of our laird's lady and Bridgett," Fergus admonished him.

Clarence apologized to both women before adding, "I have Thomas Blue-eyes with me, and Garret the fisherman. But I think they both have passed on. I cannae see me hand in front of me face."

"I be nae dead yet," came a weak voice, followed by an even weaker chuckle. "Me wife will kill me if this wound to me leg does nae."

There was much scurrying about and talking. These men had all fought hard to ensure the safety of the keep as well as Onnleigh and Bridgett. "I failed ye, m'lady," Fergus said. "I tried, I truly did. But I was overrun by a bunch of half-crazed people, all convinced ye are a witch."

"I wager we owe that to Helen, aye?" one of the men replied.

"Be there any way out of here?" Onnleigh finally asked.

The dungeon fell quiet.

"Nay, m'lady, I fear there is nae way out," Fergus finally replied. "But I am nae without hope," he quickly added. "I will find a way or make a way out of this bloody hell hole. On that, ye have me word."

His sincerity was so profound that Onnleigh actually allowed herself to believe him.

# CHAPTER 13

"*O*ch!" Bruanna exclaimed as she rubbed her hands over the brazier. "Me auld bones do nae take to the cold like they used to."

Her longtime friend, Frazier Randall, chuckled. "I happen to like yer auld bones."

Bruanna blushed as if she were a young lass. Frazier was seventy-seven years old, but you would never know by looking at him. Aside from his silver hair, and the wrinkles that lined his pale blue eyes, he looked just as strong and vigorous as he had at forty.

They had known one another for decades. At one time, they had been secretly engaged. But fate and circumstance would never allow the two of them to be together. He was, after all, a Randall. Bruanna's father would have rather eaten broken glass than to allow the two people to be wed.

"I ken ye be naught more than an old son of a whore," Bruanna cackled. "But I fear I cannae help meself. I still like ye!"

"Because I be an auld son of a whore, or in spite of it?" He asked mischievously. His pale blue eyes twinkled with mirth. Bruanna sighed in spite of herself.

"I can still make ye blush like a maiden," Frazier told her. "I think ye look right pretty when ye blush."

Bruanna swatted his knee and told him to behave. "Ye did nae complain about me dastardly ways this afternoon," he politely reminded her.

She blushed again. Aye, they'd been more than friends these past years. They'd been secret lovers. 'Twas one more reason why she prayed daily for peace between their clans.

She was about to admonish him, albeit only halfheartedly, when someone began to pound at her door.

"Bruanna!" came a harsh whisper. "Please, Bruanna, let me in!"

PERPLEXED, Bruanna got to her feet. Frazier, ever the warrior, withdrew his sword. "Were ye expectin' someone?" he asked her.

Bruanna rolled her eyes. "Nae, but I doubt it be a horde of warriors at me door. It sounds like a woman. Put yer weapon away, Frazier."

Undeterred, he kept his sword at the ready. He might be considered an auld man, but he was still a warrior at heart.

Bruanna shuffled to the door as the pounding continued. "Hold on, ye heathen!" she called out. "Hold on!"

"Bruanna, please!" the voice begged once again.

Bruanna flung open the door and stood in stunned disbelief. "Keep yer sword ready, Frazier," she said over her shoulder. "What are ye doin' here?" she asked.

Margaret MacCallen was standing on her doorstep. 'Twas never a good omen to see her or her mum.

"Please, Bruanna," she cried. "We need yer help!"

Bruanna was about to tell her where she could put her pleas for help when she noticed the tears frozen to the young woman's face. A moment later, Margaret pulled her cloak open to show her what she was holding. "Please," she cried. "Mum has gone mad, I tell ye. Mad!"

Bruanna wasted no time pulling the girl into her home. "What in the bloody hell are ye doin'?" she asked her. "Whose babe is that?"

Margaret's teeth were chattering so hard she was barely able to answer. "'Tis Nola," she answered as she warmed herself by the fire. She was bouncing from one foot to the other in an effort to warm up and keep the babe calm.

"Nola?" Bruanna whispered the child's name, wholly confused.

"I need yer help, Bruanna! Please, I need to get to Connor," Margaret pleaded with her.

In Bruanna's heart of hearts she knew Margaret was not pretending to be this distressed or upset. Nay, those were real tears in her eyes. Real fear in her voice.

"Tell me now, what has happened," Bruanna's sharp voice cut through Margaret's crying.

"Mum," Margaret began with a sob. "She has gone mad. She has the whole keep under siege. She has put Onnleigh and Bridgett in the dungeon. She ordered me to leave the babe in the fairy tree!"

Astonished, Bruanna could not believe what she was hearing. "How in the bloody hell did she get control of the keep?" Bruanna held Margaret's arms and shook her. "How?"

The story spilled from Margaret like water over the falls. As quickly as she could, she told Bruanna everything. From how they made the cows stop giving milk to how they were able to get most of the warriors away from the keep. "There be at least fifty people in the courtyard, callin' fer Onnleigh to be burned! They've built pyres, Bruanna! Pyres! I could nae leave the babe in the fairy tree. I could nae do it. I can nae allow mum to kill innocent people! Please, help me get to Connor before it be too late!"

Bruanna stood in stunned silence as she tried to make sense of what Margaret was telling her. Frazier stepped forward, sheathing his sword. "Leave the babe here, with Bruanna," he told her. "I have me horse behind the cottage."

Margaret looked up at him as if just seeing him for the first time. "Who be ye?" she asked.

"I be Frazier Randall, Aiden Randall's grand sire," he replied rather proudly. "Leave the babe with Bruanna. I will get ye to Connor."

Margaret held the babe more closely. "Nay!" she exclaimed. "Mum will scour the lands fer me when I do nae return. She will nae stop until she finds me and this babe. I must take her with me."

Frazier took another step forward. Margaret spun around as if to protect Nola. "The only way ye will get this babe out of me hands is by killin' me," she told him. "And if we do nae hurry, mum will kill us all. She will stop at nothin' to get what she wants. *Nothin'.*"

Bruanna placed a wrinkled hand on Frazier's arm. "I fear she speaks the truth, Frazier. I have kent Helen since the day she was born. Never a more evil woman have ye met."

Frazier glanced at Margaret, expecting an admonishment from her. Bruanna had, after all, just insulted the young woman's mother. Margaret, however, said not a word.

He looked at Bruanna. "Will ye be safe here?" he asked, placing his arm on her shoulders.

Bruanna smiled up at him. "Aye, I will be safe. Ye just worry about gettin' to Connor before Helen makes good on her promise."

IN NO TIME AT ALL, Bruanna had a small bundle packed for Frazier and Margaret's journey. She gave them extra blankets, bannocks and cheese, and all but pushed them out the door.

Frazier held the babe while Margaret mounted his gray gelding. As soon as she was settled, he handed her the babe and climbed up behind her. He took time to wrap the extra blankets around them before kicking the flanks of his horse.

"I ken a short cut to the keep," he told Margaret. "It will still take us several hours, but we will get there."

Margaret swiped away more tears. "Will yer horse be able to carry both of us?"

Frazier laughed. "I'd wager both me legs that he will," he replied with a chuckle. "This be a fine Randall steed ye be sittin' on. He will get us there, lass. He will get us there."

Margaret felt only mildly relieved at his proclamation. For a long while she remained quiet, her mind racing, her heart heavy with dread. She knew she was taking a tremendous risk by defying her mother. Once Helen realized Margaret wasn't coming back, she would be outraged. The woman would not hesitate to let go of the secret she had been holding on to for the past seven years. Nay, she would tell anyone and everyone the whole sordid truth.

And Margaret would be ruined. Of that, she had no doubt at all. People would never look at her the same. Nay, they would undoubtedly whisper about her sins, gladly taking part in spreading the ugly, sordid gossip from one person to the next.

She knew 'twas nothing less than she deserved. For years, she'd been at the mercy of her mother, doing her bidding, doing everything she could to keep her mother from speaking about it to anyone.

In the beginning, she had hated being so ugly and mean to her clanspeople. She despised herself for it.

For that first year after her father's death, Margaret ate only enough to survive. She slept very little, haunted by nightmares born out of her mother's sick promises.

As time wore on, it simply became easier to do her mother's bidding than to fight against it. Doing as she was told was better than the beatings, better than the threats her mother hurled at her like heavy rocks. *Do ye truly wish me to tell everyone what ye've done?* Her mother would taunt. *I can live with the truth. Can ye?*

Margaret wasn't even certain what the truth actually was any more. At least, she hadn't until she saw it staring back at her in the form of the maniacal look in her mother's eyes. 'Twas then, in that moment, when Helen was ordering her to kill this sweet, innocent babe, that Margaret realized the last seven years were naught more than one giant jumble of lies. At least most of it was.

Connor had no desire to marry her, no matter how many times Helen proclaimed it. Onnleigh was no more a witch than Margaret. While 'twas true Margaret was jealous of her, of how easily Onnleigh was able to steal Connor's heart, she wished her no true ill will.

And no matter how much her mother believed it, killing this babe or Onnleigh or anyone else was not going to force Connor's hand. It would not force him into a marriage with Margaret. Nay, if anything, those acts would only infuriate him. To the point he was very likely going to kill Helen for what she had done. If her instincts were correct, she'd be hanging right alongside her mother.

~

"I BE SORRY," Bridgett whispered in the dark. Her stomach was growling and she felt guilty for it.

Onnleigh couldn't have eaten if a feast had been set before her. Her mind was everywhere else but on food.

"How long do ye think we've been here," Bridgett asked, trying to ignore her hunger. She scooted closer to her friend. If she didn't stop, she'd be sitting on her lap.

"I dunnae ken," Onnleigh replied. Her voice was scratchy from all the crying. Her lip stung from the tears that had fallen into the cut.

The dungeon had grown eerily quiet. The imprisoned and injured men had talked for a long while. Each of them coming up with a more gruesome way in which to take the lives of Darwud, Helen, Margaret, and anyone else who had aided in the taking of the keep. After a time, they grew weary and quiet.

Onnleigh was beyond exhausted. Her arms and legs felt leaden, her heart just as heavy. For hours, as she had wept, she prayed that God would watch over Nola, that He would somehow keep her safe.

Closing her eyes, she rested her head on Bridgett's shoulders. The overwhelming sense of sorrow continued to envelope her. 'Twas a suffocating sensation, as if she were being held under water. Sounds were muffled, adding to the ominous air of the darkened dungeon.

Her thoughts turned to Connor and what he might be doing right now. It had to be close to the midnight hour, but 'twas impossible to tell. Chances were strong that he was still in deep negotiations with the Randall laird.

Would he somehow sense that she was in danger? Did he love her as much as he had loved his first wife, Maire? She supposed it no longer mattered, for she'd be dead before he returned.

Swiping away her tears, she closed her eyes and prayed that God would find some mercy and let her death be swift and as painless as possible.

Connor. Her thoughts kept turning to him. Aye, she knew he loved her and wanted her for his wife. The only comfort she could take at the moment was knowing that he would mourn her death. 'Twas a silly idea, she knew, but somehow, it did bring her a small measure of solace in this her darkest hour.

*Connor, I ken ye cannae hear me, but oh, how I wish ye were here. I be afraid, Connor. Verra afraid. Nola be lost to us now. Margaret took her away and set her in the fairy tree. Me heart has shattered, Connor. I cannae live without me babe.*

*I hope ye avenge our deaths, my love. But do nae mourn long fer me. I want ye to find another who ye can love. Someone who will nae bring ye the shame I have. I be so sorry. So verra sorry.*

FRAZIER'S ESTIMATION on how quickly they would arrive at his keep was spot on. He had also not exaggerated the agility or capability of his gray steed.

He had to slow their pace as they made their way through a dense forest. 'Twas a black as pitch, the tall evergreen trees blocking out most of the night sky. Margaret had no idea how the man could see in such darkness. Oddly enough, she did not feel afraid. At least not of him or their current predicament.

But whenever the image of her mother popped into her mind, ripples of fear trickled up and down her spine.

There were many times she wanted to scream at Frazier to go faster, but she had to trust that he knew what he was doing. Just how or why he was at Bruanna's, Margaret didn't ask. She was simply grateful that he had been. When she thought of what might have happened … she shuddered and drew the blanket around her more tightly.

Ahead, she saw faint glimmers of light flickering through the thick branches. Frazier must have seen them as well, for he kicked the flanks of his horse and yelled. A few rapid heartbeats later, they were bursting through the trees.

"Open the gate!" Frazier called as they sped across a small glen. The horse did his best to trudge through the deep snow as fast as he could. "Open the gate!" Frazier called out once again. They stomped across a worn path, heading toward the gates of the Randall keep. Margaret held Nola so close that the babe startled from her sleep and began to wail.

"Open the bloody gate!" He yelled. "'Tis me! Frazier Randall!"

# CHAPTER 14

*A*iden Randall felt he was a good judge of character. Most men were as easy for him to read as a sailor reads the stars. He had been raised to believe that there was at least a little bit of larceny in everyone. However, he didn't think that rule applied to Connor MacCallen.

Since MacCallen's arrival the night before, Aiden had been doing his best to size the man up and figure out what his weaknesses were. Was he prone to violence? Anger? Was he a vengeful or sardonic man? Could he be easily bribed? After spending the better part of the day with him, he realized Connor was very much like himself: God, family, and clan came first, above all other things. Nothing was as important as those three.

"I am just as tired of these border raids as ye," Connor told him. They were sitting by a roaring fire in Aiden's gathering room. They were, of course, surrounded by a dozen each of their finest warriors. Even if he couldn't see a weakness or vice in the MacCallen chief, that did not mean he could trust him fully. Trust must be gained, through time, patience and business.

Aiden kept his clan's current state a closely guarded secret. To the outside world, it might look as though they were flourishing, but in truth, they were as close to being impoverished as an Edinburgh orphan. "I believe we owe most of those raids to the McCrearys," Aiden replied as he took a sip of the fine whisky Connor had brought as a gift. He wished his own clan could make something just as smooth.

Connor nodded in agreement. "If the rumors I have heard of late are correct, the McCrearys have also come to ye to arrange an alliance."

Aiden liked his straightforward manner. "Aye, 'tis true they have."

Connor studied him out of the corner of his eye for brief moment. "Me thinks that if ye had already decided to align yourself with them, I would nae be here."

Aiden chuckled softly before replying. "Aye, ye would reckon correctly," he said. "I trust the McCreary as much as I trust an Englishman."

They were laughing over his jest when one of Aiden's men came bursting into the room. "Aiden!" he shouted as he raced toward him. "Yer grandsire has just come through the gate."

'Twas the seriousness of the young man's tone that made Aiden and Connor shoot to their feet. Aiden didn't have time to inquire as to why this was such important news.

"He has a lass with him from the MacCallen clan. She has their laird's babe. She says their clan is under siege."

Aiden watched as the color drained from Connor's face. A moment later, his dread and worry was replaced with a fury so great, Aiden thought the man's head would explode. His brother Ronald looked just as furious as he came to stand beside his brother.

"Frazier is bringin' her in now," the young man said as he fought to catch his breath.

Believing it must be Onnleigh who had brought Nola here, Connor headed to the door. Blood rushed in his ears as his heart pounded against his breast with worry.

With Ronald at his heels, Connor froze in his tracks when Frazier came in. Margaret was right behind him.

BALLING HIS HANDS INTO FISTS, his lips pursed into a hard line, it took every bit of himself not to lash out at Margaret. He took in a slow, deep breath, fully prepared the break her neck if this was some kind of nefarious plot she and her mother had put into motion.

"Connor," she cried out as she rushed toward him.

He could see that she had been crying, because of her red, puffy eyes and tear-stained cheeks. That was wholly out of character for her. Margaret never cried. At least not real tears.

When she handed Nola to him, he felt her hands shake. 'Twas as confusing a moment as he'd ever experienced. Still, he could not shake the burgeoning anger. "What in the bloody hell are ye doin' with me daughter?"

As she fought to catch her breath, the words tumbled out so quickly, 'twas difficult to understand at first. "I could nae stop her this time," she told him. "She wanted me to leave Nola in the fairy tree, but I could nae do that."

His head began to spin. "Where is Onnleigh?"

"Mum has locked her and Bridgett in the dungeon. She has everyone in an uproar. She's going to try her as a witch!" There was no hint of deception. The tears she was shedding were real. His stomach rolled at the thought of Onnleigh being tossed into his own dungeon.

Ronald looked fit to be tied, his jaw clenched, his fingers quaking with fury. He was so furious he could not speak just yet.

"Darwud and a few others be helpin' her. They lied and told the rest of yer men that ye had been attacked comin' to see the Randall. There was a call to arms, and almost all the men left," she explained. Panic-stricken, she pleaded with him to return home at once.

"Mum has control of the keep!"

*HELEN HAS control of my keep?* There were too many questions and not enough time to ask them. His head continued to swim with a blend of rage and trepidation he had never felt before.

Aiden stepped forward to offer his help. "Ye can leave her and yer babe here," he suggested. "I will gather me men to help ye."

A large part of him wanted to decline Aiden's offer. But Onnleigh's life was at stake. He'd call on the devil himself in order to save her.

"They killed so many people, Connor," Margaret admitted. "They threw the survivors in the dungeon. Fergus, Darrin, and I dunnae ken how many others."

Nola's soft whimpers had turned to outright crying.

"I gave her bits of bread on the way, but she needs milk," Margaret told him. "I did nae have any milk. I did nae ken what to do. I did nae ken what to do."

She was positively grief-stricken, her eyes filled with guilt and torment. Connor had never seen her like this before. Nay, this was not playacting. Mayhap he was seeing the real Margaret for the very first time. He glanced at his brother and realized Ronald was thinking much the same thing.

Aiden ordered someone to wake his cook and to bring milk for the bairn and to find some clean nappies. He was not without experience when it came to babes. While he wasn't a father himself, he had nine nieces and nephews, a few of which he had helped raise.

His next order was to have his men ready themselves for battle.

All the while, Connor was doing his best to comfort his daughter as he tried to make sense of everything.

Pushing aside his fear and dread, he thanked Aiden for his help. In his heart, he knew that if anything happened to Onnleigh, he would never forgive himself. He knew she had been worried about being left alone. He had foolishly believed she was safer with his clan than here.

"If I return without this babe, Onnleigh will kill me," he muttered.

Ronald spoke for the first time. "Then ye best nae return without her," he said.

Aiden studied both men briefly. "I would hate to try to gain a peace accord with the woman who has taken over yer keep." His attempt at levity fell on deaf ears.

"Trust me," Connor said as he put Nola against his shoulder, "that woman will nae live to see the end of the morrow."

WITHIN THE HOUR, Nola had been fed, changed, and wrapped in dry blankets. Aiden's cook supplied them with a few flagons of goat's milk and enough nappies to see her through to her old age.

Connor's men weren't quite sure what to think of Aiden's men or his offer to assist. His brother Ronald was equally plagued with doubts. He pulled Connor aside and asked, "How do we ken Aiden is nae in cahoots with Helen?"

'Twas not necessarily an unintelligent question. The timing of Aiden's request for a meeting fit a little too well with Helen's despicable plan. "Aye," Connor replied in a low voice as he watched Margaret closely. "I thought that verra thing."

"Then why take his offer of help?"

"'Tis sometimes necessary to keep yer enemies close, Ronald," Connor whispered. "Besides, if I am going to have to storm me own bloody keep, I will need as much help as I can get. I do nae think that Aiden is workin' with Helen."

"How can ye be so certain?" Ronald asked with a dubious frown.

"Me gut, Ronald. Me gut tells me Aiden wants peace with us as much as I do. I have nae gotten the sense that he is disingenuous or plottin' against me."

Ronald shook his head. "I pray to God ye're right."

Connor offered up his own silent prayer that his instincts about Aiden Randall were correct. He also prayed for God to keep his Onnleigh safe.

*Please, Lord, let me get to her in time.*

'TWAS IMPOSSIBLE TO TELL THE time of day. The only lit torch had gone out hours ago. There was not a window anywhere in the depths of the dungeon.

Time no longer mattered to Onnleigh. She had dozed off and on throughout what she assumed was the night. Her thoughts had gone from wanting to kill Helen with her bare hands, to wanting nothing more than to die.

Bridgett did her best to keep Onnleigh's spirits up, but what was the purpose? No one had come for them. Deep down, she was certain no one had stopped Margaret from placing Nola in the fairy tree.

Try as she might, she could not get the image of her crying daughter out of her mind. How betrayed must Nola have felt when she cried and no one came to comfort her? She must have been terrified beyond imagination. Onnleigh had never let her babe cry for more than a moment or two.

There was naught left of her heart now, for it had turned to dust hours ago.

*Nola, please fergive me,* she had chanted silently all through the night. *Please fergive me fer nae keepin' ye safe. I will ne'er fergive meself.*

The only thing that brought her any comfort was knowing that before this day was done, she would be dead. Hopefully 'twould be sooner rather than later, because she did not know how much more of this agony she could withstand.

*I will be with ye soon, love. That is if God can fergive me fer nae doin' more to save ye.*

The stillness of the dungeon was broken by the sound of the main door scraping against the stone floor. What was left of Onnleigh's heart seized at the sound.

Bridgett heard it as well and shot straight up. She'd been leaning against Onnleigh for God only knew how long.

"Mayhap that be Ronald," Bridgett whispered.

Onnleigh couldn't allow herself to believe that for a moment.

A stream of light spilled in, growing larger as someone approached. 'Twas Darwud, looking just as smug as he had when he'd left them here hours before. With him were two men Onnleigh did not recognize. Both appeared to be in their fifties, with thinning hair and stomachs that bespoke of never having missed a meal.

"Up with ye," Darwud ordered as he stood by the cell door. "'Tis time fer yer trial."

Bridgett scurried away, refusing to obey his command. "To the devil with ye, Darwud!" she screamed at him.

"She has nae done anythin'!" Onnleigh cried out. "Leave her be!"

Darwud motioned for the shorter of the two men to unlock the door. "She be yer good friend, aye?"

The man pulled a set of keys that dangled at his belt and quickly unlocked the door. He stepped aside, letting the keys fall back against his leg.

"What does that matter?" Onnleigh asked as she wrapped her arms around Bridgett. "'Tis me Helen hates, nae Bridgett!"

In a few short strides, Darwud was inside the cell, pulling Onnleigh to her feet. His taller cohort stepped in and grabbed Bridgett about her waist. The two women kicked and screamed, fighting with all their might to free themselves. But 'twas to no avail.

"Settle down," Darwud yelled at them. "Ye can fight all ye want, but ye'll soon both be burnin' at the stake."

"I hate ye!" Onnleigh screamed as she scratched and clawed at his face.

Furious, he balled his hand into a fist and slammed it into her cheek, sending her to the stone floor. Dots of bright white light floated in front of her eyes, her cheek throbbing in rhythm with the blood rushing in her ears.

Bridgett heard Onnleigh scream and Darwud's laughter. A low roar rent the air. 'Twas the other prisoners, voicing their anger, making promises to kill Darwud at the first opportunity.

Grabbing her upper arm, Darwud yanked her to her feet once again. Her stomach recoiled at his touch, the nausea overwhelming. Using bits of rope, the men tied the young women's hands behind their backs. Darwud tied Onnleigh's so tightly it burned.

How could she have ever believed he was a kind, sweet man? How could she have been such a fool?

And how could she have put any faith in the belief that she belonged here?

DOWN THE DANK corridor he dragged her. She was momentarily blinded by the bright light that shone in through the windows that lined the winding staircase. Squinting against it, she tried to steady the woozy feeling building in the pit of her stomach.

Bridgett and the other man were right behind them. Bridgett cursed him to the devil, along with everyone else who had helped in this charade.

Onnleigh didn't believe fighting would do them a darned bit of good. These people were hell bent on seeing her dead.

Down a narrow hallway and into the gathering room they dragged the two women. Onnleigh couldn't stifle the gasp when she looked around. At least thirty people were gathered, men and women of all ages. Some had even brought their children to witness the farce. They murmured curses and tossed the word *witch* around like pebbles. Each word stung Onnleigh to her core. *How could ye believe this about me?*

She shivered involuntarily as she was brought before one of the long tables. Helen sat behind it, looking for all the world like a queen. Her crimson gown was adorned with silver threads, her hair covered with a bejeweled headpiece, gossamer fabric cascading down her back.

Bridgett was shoved over to stand beside Onnleigh. Bridgett scowled at Helen, making no effort to hide the contempt she felt for the older woman. Helen ignored her.

"Onnleigh *ingen* Grueber and Bridgett *ingen Comnal,*" Helen began. "Ye have been brought forth this tribunal having been accused of witchcraft."

Bridgett openly scoffed. "Tribunal?" she asked, thoroughly

disgusted. "What power do *ye* have to call forth anyone? Ye be nae the chief nor chatelaine!"

"With Connor gone, it falls to me—"

Bridgett cut her off. "It falls to Fergus," she said. "But ye have him locked away in the dungeon. Ye be naught but a mean, vengeful, horrid auld hag! To the devil with ye Helen MacCallen! To the devil with ye, I say!"

Helen was undeterred. With a slight inclination toward Darwud, she encouraged him to grab a handful of Bridgett's hair and yank her to her knees. Bridgett let out a yelp, more out of anger than pain.

"'Twould behoove ye to remain quiet, ye little witch," Darwud seethed into her ear. "Else I will gag ye."

Resting her palms on the table, Helen looked around the room. "Do ye see? Onnleigh has turned our sweet Bridgett into a raving lunatic."

The crowd voiced its agreement rather loudly, with jeers and hisses.

Onnleigh had yet to take her eyes off Helen. If she could, she would fling herself across the table and strangle the life out of the woman.

"What right do ye have to do this to me? To us?" Onnleigh finally found the strength to speak.

"'Tis me right as the former chatelaine's mother to see to it that the keep runs smoothly and that all evil is expunged from it," Helen replied. Turning her attention back to the crowd she said, "Ye have all heard the evidence against these two women."

"What evidence?" Onnleigh challenged. "We have a right to hear this evidence."

Helen rolled her eyes. "Within the past few days, dozens of milk cows have quit giving milk. Chickens have been found dead, with their heads chopped off. And just yester morn, a goat was found hanging from a tree. Its heart was missing."

"And what evidence do ye have that 'twas I who did any of those things?"

Helen quirked a brow, looking rather victorious. "Then ye do nae deny it?"

"Of course I deny it!" Onnleigh exclaimed. "We have done none of those things and ye verra well ken it. I am merely askin' to know what evidence ye have that 'twas I or Bridgett who did these things."

Unswayed by Onnleigh's plea of innocence, Helen continued with her accusations. "'Twas me daughter Margaret who saw ye take the heart from the goat while it was still livin'."

Onnleigh knew 'twas a lie. Every bit of it. She turned around to search for Margaret. Oddly enough, she was not present. "Where be she?" Onnleigh asked no one in particular. "Where be the woman who accuses me?"

She saw it then, a flicker of something in Helen's eyes. What it was, she could not readily name. Was it fear? Anger? Whatever it was, it made Onnleigh begin to question everything that was taking place.

"She is ill," Helen said.

Onnleigh knew at once she was lying. Just how she knew, she couldn't guess. But she could feel it in her bones. "Ill?" she asked. "Did she get a cough when she put Connor's daughter in the fairy tree?"

An audible gasp ripped through the room. Helen shot to her feet, looking wounded. "Do ye see how she lies so easily?" she asked the crowd. "Aye, Margaret took ill and 'twas all yer doin'. Ye cast a spell on her, I am certain of it. And if me sweet Margaret dies, her death will be on yer hands!"

Not for a moment did Onnleigh believe Helen's outrage. Glancing over her shoulder at the crowd, she knew there was not a thing she could do to change any of their minds. Their minds were twisted with the hunger for revenge.

Helen leaned over the table, looking directly into Onnleigh's eyes. "Ye have been found guilty of witchcraft," she said. Onnleigh could see she was fighting hard to regain her composure. "As have ye, Bridgett *ingen* Comnal. Ye are both hereby sentenced to death."

The crowd cheered as they waved their fists in the air. "Burn the witches! Burn the witches!" Their thirst for blood made Onnleigh's run cold. Her skin turned to gooseflesh when Helen gave Darwud the order to strip them down to their chemises.

Bridgett fought like a cat-o'-mountain, scratching and clawing at the two men who were stripping her dress away. She managed to scratch one of the men along his cheek.

Onnleigh stood numb. She had no fight left in her. Once again, she was alone in this world, just as she had been as a little girl when Helen beat her out of the walls of the keep.

Darwud tore at her dress, ripping the bodice with his bare hands. With a few hard yanks, he had the dress in shreds, pooling at her feet. Using his dirk, he cut the sleeves away so he would not have to untie her hands. Undoubtedly he worried she would claw at him again if she had the opportunity. Her slippers were removed next, as were Bridgett's.

'Twas simply one more form of degradation of the many she had endured in her lifetime.

Instead of feeling sorry for herself, she chose instead to think of Nola. Sweet, sweet Nola. *It will nae be long now, my sweet babe, and I will have ye in my arms once again.*

CONNOR COULD NOT BELIEVE what he was seeing. Hundreds of his people were standing outside the walls of the keep, demanding entry. His warriors were lobbing arrows over the top of the wall at the people inside. Another group of some twenty men, were in the process of using a battering ram to gain entry.

"Heave!" one of the men shouted. *Thump!* Came the sound of the heavy wood against his iron gate. "Heave!" Thump.

In all his life, he never imagined he would have to lay siege to his own keep. 'Twas the darkest of days.

Kicking his horse into a full run, he led the charge, racing with his own men and Aiden's across the glen and down the hill. One of his warriors spotted him and came running. "Connor! Connor!" he yelled as he trudged through the deep snow.

'Twas Seamus MacDonald and he looked mightily glad to see him. "Thank God ye be here!"

Connor pulled reign, bridle and bit jangling, his horse baying and stomping just inches from Seamus.

"They have all gone mad!" Seamus shouted over the din. Quickly, he tried to explain to Connor what was happening. "By the time we realized 'twas a ruse to get us away from the keep, we came back as quickly as we could," he said in a rush. "Whoever be workin' with Helen refuses to allow us back in. We spent half the night chopping down a tree big enough to use as a battering ram."

He caught sight of Braigh then, across the way. 'Twas he who was yelling the order to 'heave'. "Braigh!" he called out to him, but he could not be heard over the shouts of his people.

"There be less than eighty by my estimation," Seamus told him. "But it be enough to keep us out while they do their dirty work!"

Connor clenched his jaw, his muscles coiled, ready to kill. He would take no prisoners this day. "Kill them if ye must!" he shouted.

The battering ram was beginning to work. He watched as the thick, heavy iron hinges started to pull away from the stone wall. Turning back to Ronald, he gave the order to pull forward. "Get inside that bloody wall now!"

There was no need to ask again.

Just as Connor, Ronald and the rest of the men reached the wall, the gate finally gave way. Blood rushed in Connor's ears. His head buzzed blinding him with fury.

They rode fast and hard across the fallen gate and into the courtyard. 'Twas utter mayhem inside. People were chanting *Kill the Witch! Burn them! Kill them!*

But when those people heard the thunder of hoofbeats, their thirst for death quickly faded away. With one look at all the warriors racing over the fallen gate, they all began to scurry, like rats from a sinking ship.

His heart nearly stopped beating when his eyes fell on the middle of the courtyard.

Two pyres. One for Bridgett. One for Onnleigh.

A LOW HUM began to build inside his head. In a matter of moments, he could hear nothing else but the deep, steady hum. Unparalleled rage erupted within him.

As he raced toward the pyre, he caught a glimpse of Helen. "Helen!" He called out to her as he pulled rein. The front legs of his mount dug into the muddy earth.

She looked up, right into his eyes just before she set Bridgett's pyre ablaze with a torch.

"Stop her!" he called out to anyone who could hear him.

Braigh was on foot, heading toward the woman, but he could not get to her in time. She tossed the lit torch onto the sticks and branches before scrambling away. Thick, acrid smoke billowed heavenward. Connor lost sight of Helen and his brother.

Bridgett was crying, screaming for God's mercy as the flames licked at her feet. As Ronald and Connor raced toward them, he caught sight of Fergus. The man was pulling the burning wood away from the pyres with his bare hands.

Panic hit Connor when he saw Darrin limping toward the pyre with a dirk in one hand. He unsheathed his sword and raced forward, fully intent on taking the man's life. The entire world seemed to slow down.

Darrin walked directly into the burning embers and began to saw away at the ropes binding Bridgett to her pyre. At seeing what Darrin was doing, Fergus removed a dirk from his belt and began to cut Onnleigh free.

Darrin lifted Bridgett into his arms and spun, trying to get away from the flames and smoke. Coughing, sputtering, he slid down from the pyre.

With his reins betwixt his teeth, Ronald leaned over in his saddle and lifted Bridgett into his arms. The smoke was so thick, he could barely see where he was going.

Connor's steed stomped and clawed at the earth, screaming in fear as the smoke around them intensified. Flames continued to lick upward like fingers rising from the bowels of hell.

His eyes burned, his throat stinging from the heavy smoke. Fear draped over his heart when he lost sight of Onnleigh and Fergus.

"Fergus! Onnleigh!" he shouted, coughing and hacking.

His horse was growing more and more fearful of the close proximity to the flames. Connor gave a tug on the reins, pressed his knees against its stomach, willing the beast to settle. He still could not see Onnleigh. His heart continued to pound against his breast. *Please God, nay!*

He was just about to dismount when Fergus appeared like a giant, ancient god through the smoke. Onnleigh was draped in his arms, her head lolling lifelessly.

Connor pulled his horse closer, reaching his arms out. With a grunt, Fergus handed her up to him. "Give me yer sword!" Fergus shouted. "And get the lass out of here!"

Holding Onnleigh tightly to his chest, Connor turned his mount around and headed back over the broken gate. Until the keep was under control, he'd not risk so much as a hair on her head.

RONALD AND BRIDGETT were halfway to Bruanna's cottage when he brought his horse to an abrupt stop. Bridgett hadn't stopped crying or shivering. Gently, he wrapped his cloak around her and pulled her to his chest.

"Why have we stopped?" she asked between sniffles. "Where are we?"

It took every bit of energy he had not to come undone in front of her. When he saw her on the pyre, his world stopped spinning.

Taking in a deep, fortifying breath, he finally had the wherewithal to look into her eyes. They were brown, with little flecks of gold. Her cheeks were red from crying, smudged here and there from the ravages of the pyre. Her chemise was nearly black, as were her fingers and arms. His heart splintered.

Tenderly, he lifted her chin with a crooked finger. The words he wanted to give to her wouldn't come. They were lodged in his throat, right along with his heart. Without so much as a by-your-leave, he bent low and pressed his lips to hers.

They were just as soft as he had imagined they would be. Softer than the petals of the finest roses. For a long moment, she did not move. He imagined he had frightened her to such a point that she was frozen in place. But a few fluttering heartbeats later, she was returning his kiss with a fervency he didn't think possible.

A warmth he'd never felt before exploded deep within his chest. As much as he would have enjoyed kissing her for the next day or two, he knew he had to get her to Bruanna's home as swiftly as possible.

Reluctantly, he broke the kiss and took in another deep, fortifying breath. "When I learned ye had been taken prisoner, I made myself a promise."

"Promise?" she asked, uncertainty filling her pretty brown eyes.

"Aye," he replied, his voice catching. "I promised myself that if I got to ye in time, I would kiss ye. And I would nae stop kissin' ye until the day I took me last breath on God's earth."

Those pretty eyes grew as wide as trenchers before they filled with more tears. "I knew ye would come for me," she told him, her voice cracking. "I told Onnleigh ye would."

His lips curved into a tender smile. "'Twould have taken God's own hands to keep me from ye."

They sat staring at one another for a long moment. When she started to shiver again, he tapped the flanks of his horse. After a while, Bridgett asked the question that was lingering in the air. "What does yer promise mean, exactly?"

He chuckled and gave her a gentle hug. "It means that as soon as I can find a priest, ye and I will be married."

Had the circumstances been anything other than what they were, Bridgett would have insisted on a proper proposal. She would have

demanded he profess his love for her for now through the end
of time.

But she had been in love with this man for as long as she could
remember. While it had taken much to get Ronald to this point — her
nearly being killed — she was glad he had finally come to his good
senses.

Later, she would insist he give her the words.

CONNOR HELD Onnleigh as close to his chest as he could. With his
plaid draped around her, he rubbed her arms, begging and pleading
with her to open her eyes.

"Be she all right?" Aiden asked him as he stood near the fallen gate.

"I dunnae," Connor replied with a shake of his head.

"Go," Aiden told him. "We will take care of things here."

"Find Fergus," Connor told him as he surveyed the destruction that
had befallen the courtyard. Men had already formed a bucket line
from the well. They were pouring water on the pyres. He prayed none
of the embers would spread to other buildings. "He will help ye," he
said, his gut filled with disgust and shame.

Aiden gave him a nod of understanding. A moment later, Connor
took off like a bolt of lightning. 'Twas odd, asking a man who until
two days ago had been a complete stranger to him. He prayed he'd not
regret his decision to accept the man's help.

Once they were a goodly distance from the keep, Connor slowed
his pace so that he might direct his full attention to the woman lying
so still in his arms. Covered in soot and ashes, her cheeks smudged,
her chemise torn and nearly black, she looked so pitiful. Seeing her
like this, unmoving, barely breathing, reminded him of when Maire
died. It felt as though he'd just been kicked in the gut by an angry
horse.

Flashbacks to that awful day, when Maire lay dying in his arms,
nearly caused his undoing. Always a beacon of hope, brightness and
all things good she had been, before God called her home. Their babe

had come early, far too early and Maire's body simply couldn't handle it.

And like that, she was gone.

His eyes filled with tears of regret and sorrow. Looking down at Onnleigh, so helpless, so light in his arms, he begged and pleaded with her again. "Please, Onnleigh, wake up! Open yer eyes, love. Please, open yer eyes."

When she did not respond, he tore across the land, heading for his grandminny's home. His worry grew with each pounding hoofbeat, with each step farther away from his keep.

He prayed that God would not take Onnleigh away from him. *Nae like this, Lord. Please, nae like this. She deserves so much more.*

His gut was a blend of fury, betrayal, and sheer guilt. Fury towards those who would try to bring harm to innocents like Onnleigh, Bridgett, and Nola. 'Twas the highest form of betrayal he could imagine.

Though 'twas so cold he could see his own breath, his tunic was soaked in sweat. His heart pounded as if he'd just run all the way across Scotia.

His only concern at the moment was for Onnleigh's safety.

They had just crested a small hill when she began to shiver violently. "C-cold," she muttered before she was overcome with coughing.

Connor blew out a sigh of relief. If she could speak and cough, then she would be well. He stopped quickly, pulled his arms out of his cloak and wrapped Onnleigh in it. Up ahead, not far, was his grandminny's home. He could just make out the chimney, smoke rising up against the gloomy gray sky.

Onnleigh's eyes fluttered open. For a moment, she looked at him in disbelief, as if he weren't really there. So glad he was to see her, he could not help but smile at her. "Och! Thank God!" he exclaimed joyfully as he held her close.

She began to sob, uncontrollably, holding his tunic in her fists. Connor rubbed her back doing his best to soothe her.

"They killed her!" she screamed against his chest. "They killed Nola!"

"Nay, lass, Nola be fine!"

Onnleigh shook her head as she continued to weep. "Nay, Connor! Margaret took her and put her in the fairy tree. Please, take me there now!"

"Wheest, lass," he whispered. "Our babe be at me grandminny's right now. Margaret did nae take her to the fairy tree. She found help and brought her to me at the Randall's keep."

Stunned, she lifted her head to look at him. "What?"

He smiled at her warmly. "That be right, lass. Nola be well, I swear to ye. I left her with grandminny an hour ago."

A moment passed before she broke down again. This time, she cried tears of joy and relief.

"Please, Connor, hurry!" she told him as she struggled to sit up.

"As ye wish, lass. As ye wish."

FERGUS SAW HIM FIRST.

Darwud was heading toward the gate, attempting to escape. Fergus was not going to allow that to happen.

Though his hands and arms ached and burned from the fire, he refused to let Darwud gain his freedom. Thick, acrid smoke billowed, filling the air, stinging his eyes and lungs.

"Darwud" 'Twas Red John's deep voice booming through the air.

Upon hearing his name, Darwud stopped. He took one look at the towering, red bearded man, and he turned seven shades of green from fear.

Out of the corner of his eyes, Fergus caught a glimpse of Clarence coming up from his left. Clarence's tunic gaped open, and blood oozed from the earlier cut to his stomach. Though he looked as though he were at death's door, he also looked quite determined to give Darwud his due.

Even through the heavy smoke, Fergus could see the fear in Darwud MacCallen's eyes. He watched as the young man unsheathed his sword. 'Twas a foolish move.

"Put yer weapon away, Darwud," Fergus called to him as he slowly began to approach the terrified fool. "And ye might just live to see another day." 'Twas a half truth. Fergus knew that as soon as he found out 'twas Darwud who had beaten Onnleigh, the man would not live long after.

"And let ye slice me throat?" Darwud asked, his voice catching on his fear.

Fergus shook his head. "If ye surrender, I swear to ye that I will nae slice yer throat, nor harm ye in any other way." Nay, he'd leave that pleasure to Connor.

Darwud had proven his ignorance and foolishness more than once over the past two days. But his next moved proved to be his last.

With sword drawn, he lunged at Clarence, under the misguided notion that the man was too weak to defend himself. He was quite wrong in that assumption. He also neglected to take into consideration the fierce determination set in Red John and Fergus.

Before Darwud could get to Clarence, Red John and Fergus were plunging their swords into his flesh. Red John's sword landed successfully into his gut, while Fergus's cut across his throat.

Darwud's eyes grew wide as he slowly sunk to his knees, grabbing his neck with one hand. His sword fell from his hand as blood gushed from his gaping wound.

"That be fer what ye did to Onnleigh," Red John said as he removed his sword. "This be fer what ye did to Garret the Fisherman and Thomas Blue eyes", he said before plunging the sword into Darwud's heart.

# CHAPTER 15

*B*ruanna's cottage was filled near to bursting. It had been a good number of years since she'd had this many people inside. Decades at that. It did her old heart much good to have these people here. Well, most of them anyway. She still had many doubts about Margaret who had ensconced herself in a dark corner. The young woman was doing her best not to be seen.

Onnleigh sat in a chair, wrapped up in Connor's plaid and a warm blanket Bruanna had given her. With a smile that could light the darkest of nights, Onnleigh beamed as she held her daughter close. To say she was relieved at having Nola in her arms once again, would have been a horrible understatement.

Connor shined almost as brightly as Onnleigh. He sat next to her with a protective arm draped around her. He could not stop placing kisses on Onnleigh's cheek or his daughter's forehead.

Ronald and Bridgett were huddled together on Bruanna's bed. They too were smiling, having just announced to all in attendance that they would soon be married.

Sitting at the table next to Bruanna was her dear friend, Frazier. Occasionally, she would catch him staring at her, a warm and tender smile on his lips.

"Margaret," Connor called to her.

Startled, she jumped slightly, but kept her head down.

"Margaret," Connor called to her again. "Please, come here."

Like a child who'd been caught stealing sweet cakes, she slowly made her way to the center of the room. With her hands clasped in front of her, she kept her gaze on the floor.

Onnleigh finally tore her gaze from her daughter. "I want to thank ye, Margaret."

Margaret's head shot up so fast, Bruanna was surprised it didn't hurt.

"Had ye nae defied yer mum, well, none of us would be standin' here right now."

Margaret remained quiet, her expression unreadable.

"I ken it could nae have been easy, goin' against her," Onnleigh said. "But I will be fere'er beholden to ye fer doin' so."

"I could nae hurt her," Margaret said. Her voice was naught but a whisper.

Connor was not so inclined to dismiss her previous actions so easily, but he was too happy at the moment. He would decide later what was to become of her.

The door to Bruanna's cottage flew open. Set against the backdrop of the dark gray sky, for a moment, it looked as though a bear was stepping inside. 'Twas Braigh, covered from head to toe in dark fur.

Snow swirled around his feet, the cold air chilling the space almost instantly. "Shut the door, ye daft man," Bruanna scolded him. "And come warm yerself by the fire."

Braigh did not look pleased. "Connor, Ronald," he said, keeping the door behind him open. "I need to speak with ye."

From the hard set of his jaw, the piercing glower he sent Margaret's way, Connor suspected this had something to do with Helen.

Ronald placed a tender kiss on Bridgett's lips, inducing a most contented sigh from the young girl. He whispered something in her ear. A warm blush crept up her neck, turning her cheeks a deep crimson.

"I will nae be gone long, Onnleigh," Connor said as he threw his cloak around his shoulders. He kissed her sweetly, before caressing Nola's cheek with the back of his hand. "She be a right beautiful babe, aye?"

Onnleigh nodded but cast a concerned look toward Braigh. "Braigh, how be Lorna? And her sister?"

"They both be fine," he replied gruffly, his piercing gaze still trained on Margaret.

The three men said not another word as they left the cottage.

BRAIGH WAS FURIOUS, to say the least. His nostrils flared, his brow drawn into a hard line as he took to his horse. "We found Helen," he told his brothers. "It took everythin' I had in me nae to gut her."

Connor and Ronald pulled themselves up onto their own mounts and rode beside Connor back to the keep. "Ye had me permission to kill her," Connor told him.

Braigh grunted. "I would have had she nae been holdin' a wean."

With a raised brow, Connor asked him to explain.

"I was chasin' after her and fell over the bloody gate," Braigh told him. "By the time I got to her, she had taken Mavis MacDonald's wean right from her arms. Helen was holdin' the poor boy as a shield, refusin' to put him down unless I promised she could meet with ye."

Ronald grunted his disproval. "She has no compunction on takin' someone else's life, but would use a wean to protect her own. Coward."

Aye, 'twas a most cowardly act, indeed. "Where be she now?" Connor asked.

"I threw her bloody arse in the dungeon."

"I would have gutted her along the way," Ronald stated quite firmly.

Connor believed he might have done the same. Mayhap it was best that Braigh had found her instead of himself or Ronald. In the end, he supposed it didn't matter. One way or another, Helen would pay for her crimes.

"I still find it hard to believe she was able to take over our keep with no more than fifty people aidin' her," Braigh said, still fuming.

"Had our men nae believed Ronald and I had been attacked and come after us to help, she would nae have been so successful," Connor told him.

Braigh grunted once again. "Lorna's sister was another ruse. She be fine. She had nae given birth and she was clearly nae on her deathbed. When I realized somethin' was afoot, I left Lorna with her sister and returned as soon as I could."

Connor resisted the urge to chuckle, but knew his brother was suffering. Not because he'd been lied to, but because he'd been separated from his wife.

"Ye will also be glad to ken there be nothin' left of Darwud," Braigh told him.

Connor and Ronald exchanged confused glances with one another.

"Those bruises on Onnleigh's face?" Braigh asked with a raised brow.

Aye, Connor had seen them, but he had yet to question her as to how she came by them. He'd been too overjoyed with relief to have her alive.

"She owes those to Darwud," Braigh told him. "The men who he'd thrown in our dungeon were witness to it."

Connor had never really liked nor trusted Darwud, for he knew him to be a coward as much as he was a cheat. He knew the man's proclivity for being unfaithful to his wife. But …

Clarity suddenly dawned bright in his mind. Could Darwud be the man who sired Nola?

"Fergus extends his apologies for nae allowin' ye the honor of guttin' the bloody bastard," Braigh said. "But Darwud made the mistake of takin' up his sword against Fergus."

Connor could not rightly blame Fergus for his actions. Later, when he was alone with Onnleigh, he would get the truth from her, once and for all, as to who had sired Nola. "As long as he be dead, that is all that matters," Connor told him. "I will remember to thank Fergus later."

With Ronald's help, they explained to Braigh everything they had gleaned from Margaret. By the time they reached the walls of the keep, they had finished with the telling.

"How can anyone be so evil?" Braigh asked.

A group of men had attached ropes to the iron gate and were in the process of pulling it away with a team of horses. Tiny wisps of smoke and steam billowed up from the pyres, reigniting Connor's anger. Less than two hours ago, his betrothed and her dearest friend had been tied to those pyres. Had he been delayed by even the briefest of moments, had Fergus and the men not been able to help? He had to push those thoughts aside for now, elst he might loose his mind.

'Twas only out of respect for Maire that Connor did not order Helen and Margaret to be hanged. Death, he decided, was too easy for both of them.

There was a punishment that would be far worse than death for the two women.

Helen, bound at her wrists, now stood before him in the gathering room. Aiden and a handful of his men stood at the back, quietly observing the proceeding. A dozen of Connor's warriors stood behind Helen and the two guards who had brought her up from the dungeon.

For the last quarter of an hour, he and his brothers had listened to the irrational tirade of a woman who was insane. *'Twas me right to do it,* she had repeated. *Onnleigh has bewitched ye. Me sweet Margaret loves ye. I was only lookin' out fer ye!*

Finally, he could take no more. He stood behind the long table, the same one where Helen had ordered the deaths of Onnleigh and Bridgett only a few hours before. "I have heard enough," he said, his voice low yet firm.

Helen did her best to appear forlorn and repentant. He knew she was anything but. "I am banishing everyone who helped aid ye in yer quest fer power and yer lust for revenge."

Helen apparently believed he was including herself and Margaret in that banishment. She didn't appear to be put off by the decision. Nay, he saw the flicker of relief in those evil eyes. And something else. Already she was plotting some new heinous, unspeakable plan. He was not about to give her the chance to hurt any of his family or people again.

"Ye, however, shall be ensconced at Culross Abbey for all the rest of your days."

For only the tiniest moment did she look horrified. Once again, he could see her mind working, thinking, churning likes the cogs of a pulley. "Ye will have absolutely no contact with anyone. Nae from this clan or any other. Ye will nae be allowed visitors. From sunrise to sunset, ye will do naught but what the monks direct ye to do. I be certain there will be a good deal of prayer and study fillin' up yer days, instead of plottin' and takin' revenge on innocent people."

With a nod to the guards, he ordered her removed and put back into the dungeon. She went kicking and screaming, cursing Connor, his brothers, Onnleigh, and even her own daughter.

Margaret.

Not once did she ask where her daughter was. Not once did she inquire about Margaret's well-being or what would become of her. Instead, she blamed Margaret for her demise. "That bloody whore!" she screamed. "I hope she rots along with the rest of ye!"

For a moment, Connor actually felt sorry for Margaret. He could not begin to imagine having been raised by such a hateful woman. *How could* that *woman have birthed Maire?* He doubted he would ever have the answer to that question.

BRUANNA STUDIED Margaret closely for a long while. "'Tis only because ye saved Nola that Connor has nae yet called fer yer death."

Margaret shrugged her shoulders ever so slightly. In truth, she did not care at the moment what punishment Connor might mete out. Whatever it was, it was nothing less than what she deserved. And it would pale in comparison to what her mother had in store for her.

There was no way she could explain her reasons for doing what she had done, not without revealing all of the sordid, ugly details. 'Twas doubtful any of them would understand.

"Bruanna, me thinks Margaret is feeling verra afraid right now," Onnleigh said. "I, fer one, will always be in her debt."

Margaret kept her feet firmly planted, afraid to move or say anything. In truth, she didn't want Onnleigh's gratitude. She wanted nothing but to be as far away from this place as she could get. Even if it meant Connor would order her hanged on the morrow.

"Margaret? Do ye ken *why* yer mum hates me as she does?" Onnleigh asked.

Margaret finally looked up at her. "Me mum hates everyone," she replied softly. *Includin' me.*

"Why do *ye* hate me so?"

"I do nae hate ye," she said. 'Twas the God's truth she didn't. While she might not have a strong liking for the woman, she by no means hated her. Nay, her mother had enough hatred in her heart for ten women.

"Ye certainly have an odd way of showin' it," Bridgett interjected. She was still bloody angry with her.

Margaret chose to remain quiet instead of looking at her. None of them would ever understand.

LOUISA HAD SENT someone to Bruanna's with clean clothing for Onnleigh and Bridgett, along with more goat's milk for the babe. According to the young boy, those who had invaded the keep had been caught. They learned that Fergus had been able to retrieve the keys from one of the offenders in order to affect an escape. Those men who had been held captive were now being tended to by the healer. Most were expected to live. The boy knew nothing else.

Onnleigh and Bridgett washed up as best they could in Bruanna's tiny cottage. "I imagine it will take more than a few baths to get the smoke out of our hair," Bridgett said. Onnleigh agreed.

They were exhausted, but there were too many questions and neither woman was willing to wait to get them. "How on earth was Margaret able to get to the Randall keep and back in such a short amount of time?" Bridgett asked that particular question.

Bruanna and Frazier exchanged knowing glances with one another. Deciding they would be unable to keep their friendship secret any longer, she decided to tell the young women the truth of the matter. Or at least a good part of it. There were some things a woman wanted to keep to herself.

"Frazier and I have been friends a good long while," Bruanna began. "Thank the Gods he was visitin' me yesterday when Margaret came pounded on me door."

Onnleigh and Bridgett glanced at each other before turning their attention back to Bruanna. "But I thought the Randalls were our enemies?" Onnleigh said, thoroughly confused.

"The *clans* be enemies of sorts," Frazier said. "But sometimes, a friendship can be stronger than an alliance or lack of one, betwixt clans."

Onnleigh started to ask another question, but Bruanna shot her a look of warning. She closed her mouth, deciding 'twould be best not to poke that particular beehive.

"'Twas I who took Margaret to our keep," Frazier added. "I've been usin' the same shortcut for a spell now, to come visit Bruanna."

"We will always be in yer debt," Bridgett said.

Frazier smiled fondly at Bruanna while he patted her hand. "There be naught I would nae do fer this fine woman."

Onnleigh drew her lips inward to keep from smiling when she saw the blush creep up Bruanna's face. If she did not know better, she would swear the two people loved one another. And 'twas a love that went far deeper than just a friendship.

ONNLEIGH AND BRIDGETT had climbed into Bruanna's little bed, with Nola between them. Margaret sat quietly by the fire listening to the old couple whispering to one another.

'Twas hours before Connor and his brother's returned to Bruanna's cottage. Aiden Randall was with them.

Onnleigh and Bridgett heard the men enter. They rubbed their eyes before rushing happily to their men. Margaret retreated to the corner of the cottage, once again wishing she was invisible. 'Twas difficult to gain any inkling as to what the MacCallen brothers were thinking, at least as it pertained to Margaret or her mother. Fingers of fear traced up and down her spine. There was a good possibility that Connor was going to tell her she would be hanging alongside her mother.

The small group of people whispered amongst themselves for a brief moment. Twice, she caught Onnleigh and Bridgett looking her way. Moments later, they were all stepping out of doors, leaving Margaret alone with the old couple and Aiden Randall.

It had been Aiden she had ridden with last night. She hadn't paid much attention to the man, her mind too busy with worry over what hell her mother had unleashed. Worry over whether or not they would get back in time to save Onnleigh and Bridgett.

He was as tall as Connor, thinner, but looked just as powerful. Dark hair fell well past his shoulders, a strong jaw, and a nose that had been broken at least once. His eyes, while the same pale, bright blue as his grandfather's, held an intensity that made her feel a bit uneasy.

If she weren't convinced she'd be dead at dawn on the morrow, she might have taken a bit more time to appreciate his rugged good looks.

"Have ye managed to get any sleep yet, lass?" he asked, taking a few steps toward her.

*I will be in for a verra long sleep come the morrow,* Margaret mused.

His concern was genuine, but born out of ignorance. If he knew her better, he would not have asked. "Nay," she replied.

"Have ye eaten?"

Honestly, she couldn't remember the last time she ate. Although 'twas nice to have *someone* show some sort of sincere concern for her well being, his kindness was wholly misplaced. She shook her head in reply.

She heard Bruanna let out a heavy sigh. "Margaret, if ye be hungry, I have some rabbit stew left over from me supper."

Margaret thanked her but declined the offer. Her stomach was filled with too much dread to even think about food. Besides, Bruanna looked done-in herself.

"YE JUST MADE an alliance with the Randall, and now ye want to saddle him with Margaret for the rest of his life?" Ronald was dumbfounded. "I thought ye *liked* the man."

"'Twas nae my idea," Connor told him. "'Twas Aiden's."

Ronald let out a low whistle as he shook his head in dismay. "Aiden be *choosin'* Margaret?"

"Aye, that is what I've been tryin' to tell ye," Conner said. In truth, he was just as amazed with Aiden's offer as the rest of them were.

"And did ye try to explain to him why that might nae be a good idea?" Bridgett asked.

Connor had opened his mouth to speak, but Onnleigh stopped him with a gentle hand on his arm. "Ye need to stop."

All eyes turned to her. "Margaret has many faults," Onnleigh began. "But I cannae believe she be all bad. At least nae anywhere near as bad as her mum."

Bridgett tried to speak, but Onnleigh felt it too important to not speak her mind. "She could verra well have left me daughter in that fairy tree. She could verra well have left ye and me to rot. But she did neither. Instead, she risked her own life to get to Bruanna's. She risked *everything* to keep me babe safe."

In wide eyed astonishment, Bridgett asked, "Ye have forgiven her?"

"Aye, I have. She may have helped her mum in the beginning, she may have said and done things to me before that were cruel—"

"Of course they were cruel," Bridgett argued. "Do ye nae remember her callin' ye a whore and a thief after she took yer clothes?"

"I do remember," Onnleigh said. "But now I have to ask myself *why.*"

Bridgett scrunched her brow. "Why what?"

"Why did Margaret do those things? Was it of her own choosin, or was it at her mum's direction?"

Bridgett shook her head in dismay. "What does it matter why she did those things? She be a woman full grown. She could have said 'nae.'"

Connor decided this might be a conversation left for another time. Mayhap a year or two from now. "Ladies," he said, raising his voice slightly. "None of that matters *now.* What matters is Aiden Randall wants a peace accord with us. He wants to form an alliance. He also wants a marriage betwixt our clans."

Braigh finally spoke up. "If ye ask me, I'd rather see Margaret and her mum hangin' from the wych elm trees on the hill."

Onnleigh began to object but he stayed her protests with a raised hand. "However, I must agree with Connor. A marriage between our clans would help seal the alliance. And if it means gettin' Margaret as far away from here as possible, then aye, let the Randall have her."

# EPILOGUE

*T*was just before the evening meal when the MacCallen brothers and their fiancés gathered in the tiny kirk of the keep. Warriors and clanspeople were also in attendance. Bruanna and her *friend* Frazier sat in the front row, smiling and whispering to one another. "What be goin' on with those two?" Connor asked Ronald, nodding towards his grandminny.

Ronald's brow knitted in confusion. "Our grandminny appears to be happy," he said. "When was the last time we saw her smile like that?"

Honestly, Connor couldn't remember. Oh, he had heard her laughter, seen her smile on numerous occasions. But today 'twas an entirely different kind of smile. He supposed it had something to do with Frazier Randall, but now was not the time to make any inquiries on that matter.

Connor refused to wait a moment longer to marry Onnleigh. The ceremony was only delayed long enough for Onnleigh and Bridgett to bathe and change into clean dresses. "I refuse to get married smellin' like the pyre I almost died on," Onnleigh had told him.

The events of the day proved that life was simply far too short to let anything stand in the way of true happiness. But he could not deny her request for a much needed bath.

Connor and Onnleigh exchanged their vows first. She looked regal in her burgundy wool, her dark auburn locks cascading down her back in waves. Not once did she falter in speaking her vows, in making her promise to love him and cherish him all the rest of her days. That smile, that bright, sweet smile he had grown so fond of over the past weeks, was even brighter this day.

He kissed her most passionately, to which she responded with equal fervor. Were there not two other couples to wed, Connor would have swept her off her feet and immediately whisked her off to their bedchamber.

Ronald and Bridgett were married next. Protocols and banns be damned. "I'll nae wait," Ronald told his brother.

Connor laughed outright when the priest voiced his protest. "But the banns must be read," he argued.

To which Ronald explained, "If ye do nae marry us this day, ye will be responsible fer me defilin' this fine woman."

"What do ye mean?" The priest asked with a furrowed brow.

"Because I plan on beddin' her within the next hour. Married or nae."

Bridgett didn't argue one way or the other.

The priest acquiesced immediately and married the two people. He might even have skipped reading passages from the bible. Connor supposed he wasn't too worried about Bridgett's soul.

As soon as Ronald and Bridgett were officially wed, they left the kirk in a hurry. The room erupted into laughter at watching the couple leave as if they were escaping from an English prison. Connor couldn't blame them.

Of all the bride's in attendance this day, Margaret was the only one who did not smile happily. Oh, her betrothed did, for reasons none of the MacCallens could quite understand.

But Margaret looked as though she were attending a funeral. She hadn't changed into a pretty dress, hadn't done up her hair or otherwise done anything to make it look like she was about to be married.

Connor and Onnleigh stood next to one another, acting as witnesses to the marriage. Occasionally, Onnleigh had to give Margaret a gentle nudge, for she appeared to be lost in a quiet misery.

As soon as Aiden kissed his bride, he took her by the hand. "We will be leavin' now," he told Connor. "We do thank ye kindly fer yer hospitality."

Connor chuckled, but Onnleigh looked concerned. "We thank ye as well, Randall."

Aiden shrugged his shoulders as if he hadn't truly done anything of any import.

They discussed meeting again, but not until springtime.

There had been no time to plan for a wedding feast or celebration. Mayhap in a few days, after Connor had time to set his keep back to rights.

There was far too much to be done. For one, he had people to banish. For another, there was the little matter of his grandminny and Frazier Randall that required attention.

But for now, he chose to give his bride, Onnleigh, his full, undivided attention.

# PROLOGUE

## TENDER IS THE HEART

*M*argaret wasn't given much time to fully grasp what was happening. The decision had been made. Her punishment, it seemed, was far worse than being hanged. She was being married off to Aiden Randall.

An agreement had been made betwixt the two men. Finally, after decades of considering the Randalls their enemies, they would now consider them allies.

Margaret was numb, from the top of her head, to the bottoms of her feet. She hadn't listened to half of Connor's explanation, for she was too stunned with his proclamation.

Mayhap if she explained to both men *why* she could not marry, they might be apt to change their minds. But the explanation would require bringing her dark secret into the light of day. And that was something she simply did not have the strength or courage to do.

She now stood next to Aiden in the tiny kirk not hearing much of anything the priest was saying. Although dozens of candles burned brightly, Margaret saw nothing but darkness surrounding her.

Empty. That was the best way for her to describe how she felt. Empty. Devoid of any emotion other than a stark, bleak despondency.

With a gentle nudge from Onnleigh, Margaret muttered the words

181

the priest sought from her. She simply repeated what he asked, not truly hearing the words. Most assuredly, she did not feel them, and later, she would not remember them.

Dazed and numb and empty, she went through the motions, wishing with all her might that the world would simply swallow her whole. Anything would be better than *this*.

Aiden pressed a tender kiss on her lips, but not even that could stir her from this dark, black place. If anything, she felt repulsed by his touch. If she'd had the energy to run, she would have.

No matter how Connor and Onnleigh had tried to assure her that Aiden Randall was a good man, that he would treat her well, she knew better. No man, no matter how honorable or kind, would be eager to have her as a wife if he learned her secret.

# ABOUT THE AUTHOR

*USA Today Bestselling Author*, storyteller and cheeky wench, SUZAN TISDALE lives in the Midwest with her verra handsome carpenter husband. All but one of her children have left the nest. Her pets consist of dust bunnies and a dozen poodle-sized, backyard-dwelling groundhogs – all of which run as free and unrestrained as the voices in her head. And she doesn't own a single pair of yoga pants, much to the shock and horror of her fellow authors. She prefers to write in her pajamas.

Suzan writes Scottish historical romance/fiction, with honorable and perfectly imperfect heroes and strong, feisty heroines. And bad guys she kills off in delightfully wicked ways.

She published her first novel, Laiden's Daughter, in December, 2011, as a gift for her mother. That one book started a journey which has led to fifteen published titles, with two more being released in the spring of 2017. To date, she has sold more than 350,000 copies of her books around the world. They have been translated into four foreign languages (Italian, French, German, and Spanish.)

You will find her books in digital, paperback, and audiobook formats.

Stay up to date with Suzan's App for Readers! Available for iOS, Android, and other smart devices.

Apple Store
GooglePlay

*Stay Up To Date*

www.suzantisdale.com
Email: suzan@suzantisdale.com

Tap any of the icons below to follow me at Facebook,BookBub, Instagram, Twitter, Goodreads, and Amazon.

# ALSO BY SUZAN TISDALE

The Clan MacDougall Series

*Laiden's Daughter*

*Findley's Lass*

*Wee William's Woman*

*McKenna's Honor*

The Clan Graham Series

*Rowan's Lady*

*Frederick's Queen*

The Mackintoshes and McLarens Series

*Ian's Rose*

*The Bowie Bride*

*Rodrick the Bold*

*Brogan's Promise*

The Clan McDunnah Series

*A Murmur of Providence*

*A Whisper of Fate*

*A Breath of Promise*

Moirra's Heart Series

*Stealing Moirra's Heart*

*Saving Moirra's Heart*

Stand Alone Novels

*Isle of the Blessed*

CPSIA information can be obtained
at www.ICGtesting.com
Printed in the USA
BVHW071202071221
623418BV00003B/149